FATE

By

Jason Atkinson

Table of Contents

Into The Woods	4 - 29
Small Town Brock	30 -76
Security Cop, Part 1	77 - 100
Security Cop, Part 2	101 - 138
Pete 'Funny Bone' Wells	139 - 153
Waking Forest	154 - 190

INTO THE WOODS

INTRODUCTION

It was still dark. All I could hear was the crunch of the brittle snow beneath my boots and the wind whipping through the trees.

Each breath leapt into the air and vanished as fog. My hands, which were buried inside my coat, made tight fists to try and stay warm. The chill of the morning could be felt throughout my body, especially my spine, as the frozen wind found it's a way down my neck and, ultimately, my spine.

My eyes quickly adjusted to the darkness around me, as this was not my first time up early. The trees in the distance always looked like they were hiding secrets at this time of day. The wind made the branches dance, but not an elegant dance like a ballet—more like thriller made to frighten.

The open field behind my house was the safe place in which my kids could run and play. The fence lining my property was the boundary of protection that gave me comfort. In the summertime, my children would often run and play in this field as if it were our backyard. I would sit on the back deck, sipping a cold drink and smile as they enjoyed each other's company.

Looking out over the field now, those footprints hadn't been seen in a long time. The blanket of snow, which covered the memories of their laughter, also revealed that nothing, not even a stray animal, had set foot on my property. The snow was a blanket; a fresh canvas that was yet to be stained.

Little did I know how stained it would become.

Part 1

Five years ago, summer

"Margaret, Jacob! It's time for dinner, let's go!" I bellowed from the back door.
My wife, Joanne, was sliding plates of hot, amazing food onto the dining table that overlooked our backyard, more of a field really. I was standing at the sliding glass door as I yelled. I stepped out onto the deck to try and spot my kids as they were playing and probably not listening.

It was a beautiful summer evening. Not a cloud in the sky, and the sun was in the distance, slowly setting. I leaned over the wooden railing at the edge of the deck. "Margaret, Jacob!" I yelled again. Nothing.

"I wonder where they could be?" asked Joanne, who was now approaching the deck also. Just then, a loud scream could be heard from the woods.

Chills went down my spine. It sounded like Margaret.

Joanne exploded first. "Margaret?!"

"Call the police!" I pointed to Joanne, and then I leapt over the side of the railing. It was about a five-foot drop from the deck to the grassy field below. I dropped and rolled and then ran as fast as I could in the direction of the woods where I heard Margaret scream.

I ran through the first wave of trees and began calling out for Margaret. The faster I went, the slower I became as the woods got thicker and thicker. Branches and bushes were all around me, and I could barely see what was ahead.
"Margaret, where are you?! Jacob!"

"Daddy! Don't let them get me too!"

That was the last I heard of my little girl. My vision was becoming disrupted, and my eyes were squinting to see. My breathing labored, and I couldn't call out for my baby girl. I couldn't find her. All I wanted was reach out and feel her soft hand in mine, her warm breath on my neck as I held her.

I went down to my knees, one hand on the ground and the other on a tree.

The next thing I heard was a voice from behind me. "John! John! Are you okay? Where are they?"

A hand reached my shoulder and that was the last thing I remembered. What was foggy now became dark and when it felt hard to breathe, now felt like I wasn't breathing at all. Everything was silent.

The next thing I knew, I woke up on my couch with my wife frantically looking over me, the sherriff looking down on me with concern, and flashing lights pouring into the house from outside.

"What the hell happened, John?" asked the sherriff with a head full of questions.

Part 2

"Where is Margaret? What about Jacob?" Joanne asked in sheer panic. She leaned down to me, on her knees, tears streaming from her eyes like waterfalls. She grabbed my shirt with both hands, with clenched fists she pleaded with me. "Where are my children!?" she sobbed and buried her head onto my chest.

All I could do was comfort her with my hand. No words would come that would express how I felt in that moment. I looked up at the sheriff, hoping he might have some answers, words of wisdom, anything. But now, instead of looking at me with a broken heart, he looked at me as a suspect instead.

"John, we need to have a little talk."

Joanne sat up a little and backed herself onto a nearby chair. Reaching for tissues, she wiped her eyes and blew her nose. The sherriff moved to a chair on the opposite side. John was now in the middle of a sherriff on a mission and a wife who he couldn't help.

"John, listen really carefully. I've known your family for a long time, and I don't want this to get ugly. But you need to tell me where those kids are."

"Bill!" I said in disbelief. "I was here with Joanna when I heard them scream. The first thing I did was tell her to call you!" I pointed at my wife while staring the sherriff in the eye.

"Do you remember anything before you blacked out? Anything at all that might help? I've already got search dogs on the way here."

"Umm, well no not really." I put my hand to my head as a headache began to throb. I closed my eyes from the pain, but at that moment, I flashed back to my time in the woods.

"Wait! Yes, I do remember something. It was Margaret. I couldn't see her, but I heard her."

Joanne immediately sat forward, listening in very closely. Even though she was a wreck, her eyes were pleading for a miracle.

"All I heard was, 'Daddy, don't let them get me too.' And then, I...I don't remember what happened next. Everything got fuzzy, like I was being overwhelmed by something. Next thing I knew was waking up here."

The sherriff sat back in his chair. His body language changed. Something was different. Joanne noticed it too, which is when she finally spoke.

"What is it, Bill? Do you know what happened to my babies?" Joanne was on the edge of her seat like she was playing the ponies and her horse was about to make the last turn.

Bill stood up. Uneasy, he paced by the front door. With his back turned to Joanne and me, he removed his hat and wiped his head before putting his hat back on. He turned and looked at Joanne, and then at me. We were all silent until Bill broke that barrier with four haunting words.

"This has happened before."

Part 3

Those four words alone brought me back to my full senses.

"What do you mean it's happened before? What the hell, Bill!"

The sherriff was now the one on trial and was backing up as he postured himself in a defensive position.

"Look, look," Bill said with his hands up. "It was long before you guys moved to town, and the story isn't exactly the same, but there is definitely a connection."

All of a sudden, Joanne piped up and became the authority in the room.

"You better sit down and tell us exactly what is going on, Bill, now!"

Bill simply did as he was told and calmly perched himself back in the seat. And then he began to tell a story that no one had spoken of in twenty years.

"There was an incident, here, about twenty years ago. It was just before I joined the department, but I heard about it, the whole town heard about it. It was national news for a while, at least until the next political 'thing' came along.

"A widow lived in this house with her son. He was about the same age as Jacob, ten years old. He went playing out in the woods, his mom thought nothing of it and was busy anyway. Well, that night, he didn't come home."

Bill stood up at this point as he was remembering all the horrible things.

"Our department along with Fire and some other county resources, we looked all over the woods for this boy, but we never found him. All we found was..." Bill paused as he looked Joanne right in the eye.

"All we found was some ripped up clothing that looked like something from an animal." Joanne and I both gasped and sat back a little.

"There was no blood though!" Bill said, trying to sound convincing. "But we never did find that kid. We searched for a long time. We just...didn't find him. Trevor was his name."

"Well, we can't just sit here!" I said as I stood up in protest of the already defeated sherriff.

Just then, more flashing lights could be seen from the street. Bill stood up and mumbled something on his radio.

"That's reinforcements coming, John. We have sniffer dogs now, grab something of your kids so they can get the scent."

Joanne scrambled out of the room toward the kids' bedrooms. She grabbed the first clothing item she could find from the floor and ran back.

"These should work." She held them out for the sheriff to take.

"I need you two to stay here in case they come back on their own. Take this radio so you can reach us. I'm going with the other units so we can track down and find your kids!"

Before I could argue, he was bolting out the back door. I was left standing with my wife at my side and a radio that was firing up across different departments. The room felt cold. I wasn't alone, but I had never felt more absent from the world until this moment. We were both numb from the past hour. Time was standing still and yet escaping me. I needed to hear the radio sound off that they found my kids, our kids.

Little did I know that this night would stretch on forever.

***

Present day...

I crunched through the snow to the back of my pickup. I unraveled a blanket at the back which was holding snug my shotgun and knife. I put the knife in its holder and tucked it into my coat pocket. My shotgun went over my shoulder, and my gaze moved back to the woods.

I glanced back at the house one more time as I took my first steps toward the woods. Even though it was a mere second, it flooded my head with all kinds of memories playing on a movie reel with my mind as the projector. I couldn't stop it, and it made sense. Everything that happened after that night when they went missing led to this very moment.

As I met the edge of the tree line, I took in a deep breath and stepped back into the unknown. This time, however...I would meet evil face to face.

Part 4

You might wonder after all this time, why would I go back? Why now? What was so significant that I would make myself go in there and try this again?

Part of that answer lies within the history of this place. There is a presence in these woods that pulls you in. But more of a grounding base for my return was what happened those many nights ago when the sherriff came.

Our back yard was covered in vehicles and people. Dogs were barking, different clumps of volunteers were crowding together. I could see it all from my back deck. It felt safe. I was hopeful. There was no doubt in my mind that with all this power that finding my children wouldn't be a problem. But as you know, that's not exactly how it happened.

Being in a small town meant a lot of the help were volunteers, and their training for this kind of thing was not quite adequate for what was in store for them. No one was prepared. Not even the sherriff.

They all formed a line in the field close to the tree line. Everyone was given orders to walk slowly and stay together in this one, long line. As soon as they disappeared from sight, that's when I heard it.

"Agh! No—help!" Then the sound of pistols blasting. I flinched at the sound, staring intensely at the trees for any sign of...something. Joanne came out running, grabbing me, asking what was going on.

"John, why are they shooting? What's going on? Did they find my babies?"

So many questions, I was panicking on the inside from all the confusion, and I just snapped.

"I don't know, Joanne! There's got to be at least fifty people in there searching, and you expect me to..."

I was interrupted by more screams followed by whimpering dogs. Suddenly, men were running out back to the field. Instead of stopping to see if anyone else was coming, they ran to their vehicles and took off as fast as they could.

I ran down into the yard to try and stop them, but to no avail. The second driver that flew by me stared at me. It was only a brief moment, but I felt like I was watching for a long time. The look of horror on his face made my stomach turn inside-out.

One by one, cars and trucks vanished from my home until...there was only one: Sherriff Bill. I stood by his car, watching closely. Desperately, I wanted to go in there after him, but I knew that I was far too afraid to even chance it.

It was only a minute or two when I finally heard and saw the sherriff. He didn't run out like the rest. He was on his stomach, crawling at the edge of the tree line. Even though I was petrified, I knew I had to help.

Joanne was still on the deck but ran down to the sherriff's car as I was running toward Bill. I could hear him fumbling his words, he was trying to keep crawling, but he was done. As I reached him, I collapsed to the ground so that I could grab his arms and pull.

In one last ditch effort, he looked up at me, square in the eyes, and found his words. "Don't... Don't go in there..." Trying to ignore him, I tightened my grip and began to pull.

"Noooo! Stop! Aghh!"
As I let go, I couldn't help look up as something caught my eye. When I saw its face, my body turned cold and my skin pale. I fell backward and began inching away from the trees. It never took its eyes off me. It was eating me alive with its eyes, and I felt all of it.

And then, it was gone. And Sherriff Bill, I am quite certain, died at that moment. I scrambled toward the sound of my wife's voice. She was pleading for me to come back, and when I did, she could see quite clearly something was wrong.

"John, what happened? You look like you're going to throw up."

"Joanne. Our kids aren't coming home. Those eyes...it was so big..."

"What was? What do you mean they aren't coming home?! Answer me, John!" She was smacking me on the chest, her face a mix of anger and fear.

"There's something in there, Joanne. Something horrible. It looked like a wolf, but it was too big to be a wolf. Its yellow eyes were so... petrifying. Its fur was dark and rough, and those teeth...no one could survive that."

Soon we heard radio chatter from the sherriff's car asking for an update from Bill. I got back to my senses and grabbed the radio.

"Uh, hello...this is John, you need to send someone out here."

"Where is the sherriff, John? Is anyone hurt, should I send Medical?"

I paused for a moment. I wasn't sure how to break the news, or if I should at all.

"No, no medical. Just send another unit. You have to see this for yourself."

I dropped the receiver. I sat in the passenger seat of his patrol car with Joanne sitting on the grass by the front right tire. It was dark, cold, and that feeling of being alone swept over me.

***

Present moment

Now I was about to step back into the same hell that had been haunting me these past years.

Joanne left me because she couldn't handle living there

anymore, knowing what had happened. It was too much for her. I don't blame her. I'm still not sure why I stayed. Maybe it was for this moment. Maybe I needed to see it to the end.

Why am I going back now? As terrified as I am...I just don't care anymore. I cocked my shotgun and took one more step back... into the woods.

Part 5

My heart was pounding in my chest. Fight or flight instincts told me to flee—but I couldn't, not this time.

"I'm right here! You dumb beast, come and get me!" I fired from the hip one shot. I cocked it again to load the next shell. I felt stronger now, braver.

"Come on! Come on!"

Before I saw its face, I heard the ground thud and crack. The ice broke, and snow fell from treetops. I could feel its power, and the bravery went away, but I stood my ground. As I stared into the woods, I finally saw it. Those same yellow eyes, deep with evil, its fur long and dark.

Last time, I only saw its face. This time it revealed its whole self to me. I was mortified. The closer it got to me, the larger it appeared. The beast was about fifteen feet away and I felt myself was moving backward, one little step at a time.

I was now out on the grass, and the beast stood at the edge of the woods. I raised my shotgun and pointed it right at him. Unfazed, he stood, strong and mighty, ready to kill. I fired once, it hit his front left leg, but it left the beast seemingly unscathed.

As it broke through the last line of trees and came out onto the grass, I had moved into the middle of my yard. It was now or never if this were going to end. One of us wasn't going home today.

The beast was enormous. I could see all of it. It paced a little from side to side. The head was at least two feet if not three feet tall. The legs were easily four feet long...and the body of this creature. It wasn't anything you would find anywhere else. I questioned why this creature hadn't been captured or killed or at least documented...this would make national news. I was face to face with the Loch Ness of the woods!

I lifted my shotgun to aim at the beast. It stopped and stared me down. A low, but very loud growl came from the beast as it stood there and sized me up as another one of its snacks!

It ran toward me, and I fired. It growled again, assumingly, hopefully, in pain. I cocked the gun, but I couldn't fire again. I fumbled for shotgun shells but there was no time.

Everything slowed. I could see my children. They were running in the field, I could hear their laughter as they chased each other. The sun, it was warm and inviting—but it changed.

It became dark and cold, my children faded into the darkness and instead of their giggling and laughter, I heard their haunting screams that gave me nightmares for years. I was cold. Numb.

The beast was gone. I was alone. The snow around me stained red with my blood. The morning sky was brightening as the sun was finally coming into view.

I took my final breath as I looked around. I was alone. The beast had won.

The end

SMALL TOWN BROCK

PART 1
HOPES AND DREAMS

Growing up in a small, industrial town was all about getting a free ride out with a football scholarship, or finding yourself trapped forever.

Brock, like many high-school-age boys, wanted nothing more than to escape the rust dump he had grown up in. When he wasn't practicing for football or finishing homework at the last minute, Brock was instead dreaming about the day he would escape it all. Many an evening was spent on top of what was simply called "The Hill," where Brock and friends would sneak alcohol and just calmly sit and look out over the vast nothingness.

The Hill was nice because it offered a view looking away from town. The only problem was there was nothing else around. One road, not even a real highway lead in and out of town without a lot of traffic. This one escape path wound left and right farther and farther away from Brock until you couldn't see it anymore. Brock was ready...ready to escape.

But that was high school. Brock was now twenty-two and still dreaming of escape. Believe it or not, Brock was one of the lucky ones. His dad may have been a drunk and his mom always working to afford football and everything else—but most of Brock's so-called friends ended up inside a bottle or needle, or worse: dead.

Brock ended up doing the only other thing this town had to offer with someone with no apparent talent. Factory work. For the past two years, all Brock knew was the annoyingly familiar sound of steel on steel. When he wasn't at the factory, he was back on that hill...waiting. Waiting for what, I don't think Brock even knew the answer to that question. But it wouldn't be long until he figured it out.

Seeing the way his parents were acting, now divorced, Brock at least decided to save his money as best he could. He still lived at home with his mom, who was more of a roommate anyway as she still worked long hours as a waitress. Brock lived a simple life, avoiding alcohol and his dad.

It was not a Friday. Brock waited at the bus stop like usual, chatting with some of the locals. He got on the 414 bus which took him to the other side of town. The ride itself wasn't that bad. He got to see a lot of the small town bustle and, of course, the highlight of his bus journey was when the bus picked up passengers from J-Street.

It took Brock the longest time to figure out her name. But he knew she worked at the high school doing...something. He never could pluck up the courage to say something to her. He just assumed that because he didn't have a fancy college degree like her that she wouldn't care about him. Factory workers were a dime-a-dozen. Who wanted to get to know a below average guy when you have a whole world of people to choose from?

Until it was her stop, Brock just admired her from a distance. She was short, with dirty blonde hair that went down her back. Her eyes were green, and her smile made this old town feel new. Brock was, without a shadow of a doubt, in love. But only he was in love.

After she got off the bus, it was only two more stops until Brock had to get off. Standing outside the bus, all you could hear was the sound of clanking and smashing, and the smell...that was probably the one thing he hated the most. It was a stench that you could never get out of your clothes.

Brock walked in like he did anytime, found his punch card, and clocked in for another day of work. By lunchtime, Brock had worked up quite a sweat. His work locker housed his clothes and lunch. Grabbing his food, he joined many others outside and faced away from the factory. Today, however, Brock along with many others sitting outside couldn't help but notice three monkey suit men walking inside with briefcases.

"Great...more people getting laid off again..."
Brock wasn't sure who said that, but he knew it too. The past few months had been a turmoil of hard work and fear. These men in suits always came on a Friday and at the end of the day, more people were given an envelope and told not to come back on Monday. What might have been at least an enjoyable lunch break, turned into a pit of defeat as everyone waited to see if it was their turn to hit the chopping block.

For a lot of the guys sitting there, this was all they knew. They were once "Brock," full of hopes and desires. Now, they were what Brock feared he would turn into. And for those old-timers that were given their pink slip, the local bar was the only place they had left. In some sort of sick, twisted way, that bar was the only real place in town that could afford to stay open.

As the bell rang, signaling that lunch was over, everyone slowly rose and, like droids, filed in and went back to clanking and smashing steel. It was just a matter of hours now before the managers would be calling everyone to the front of the factory. When this happened, it felt a lot like the Hunger Games, except here, they didn't have to fight to survive—they had been doing that already.

Part 2
An Unexpected Journey

Later that evening, Brock was sitting on the couch watching TV. It was pushing 8 p.m. when his mom came home, tired and worn from a long day's work. She kicked off her shoes, walked over to Brock and flopped onto the couch.

"Hey honey, how was your day?" she said while coming Brock's hair with her hand. Brock didn't say anything but instead lifted the pink slip that he was still clutching in his fist.

"Oh, Brock. I'm so sorry this happened to you. You didn't deserve that. What are you going to do now?"

"I don't know, Mom. There's no work left in this place, and we're in the middle of nowhere. I don't know how they expect anyone to survive in this town anymore—it's hopeless." Before Christine, Brock's mom, could get another word in, he stood up and walked to his room and closed the door.

She sat there, sad and frustrated by the situation. She knew he was right, but what could she do?

The next morning, Brock got up as he usually would have and made himself some breakfast. Christine was already in the kitchen, waiting for Brock with a smile on her face.

"What are you so happy about this morning?" Brock said with some disgust.

"Brock, sweetie, I know how desperately you want to leave this place. I did a lot of thinking last night, and I have made up my mind. Here..." She handed him a plain, white envelope, but it felt thick. Opening it slightly, Brock could see a pile of cash sitting inside.

"Mom, what is this? I can't take your money! You work two jobs, seven days a week and can only barely afford to survive as it is." He tried giving back the cash, but she wouldn't take it.

"Brock, I have been saving money for years. For you. It was supposed to be a college fund and although it isn't much, it's enough for you to get out of town and go live your own life, on your own terms. Take it."

Brock, now connecting the dots and realizing he could escape this hell hole of a town, thought more deeply about where he could go. But before making up his mind, he leaned over and gave his mom the biggest hug she could remember. With a tear rolling down her cheek, she hugged him right back.

Christine knew that she would be losing her baby boy, but it also meant setting him free, and that was something she needed to do for him.

Brock went into his room and, on his computer, began revisiting the sites he used to look at for when he thought he was going to leave a few years ago. Now knowing he had the money to get himself started somewhere, anything was possible. A few hours went by, and Brock was certain he had figured out the best place to go.

There was only ever one bus that would actually leave town in a day, and Brock had already missed today's bus, so he took the time to pack what he could into a suitcase and backpack. Making a few calls to look for a place to stay when he arrived, he arranged some showings and also got himself a room at a cheap hotel to hold him over while he figured out the rest.

By dinner time, Brock was exhausted from all the excitement and planning. His head was pounding and full of information and questions, but it didn't matter. 8 a.m. tomorrow morning he would be on a bus headed away from here.

Brock walked to the local diner where he knew his mom would be. It was a small place with only fifteen or so tables, but it had plenty of bar top seating available. Even though from the outside it didn't look that inviting, on the inside, it was kept up quite well, at least for a town like this.

The bell rang as he opened the door, and he saw his mom taking an order at a corner table. He walked to the bar seating and perched himself right in the middle, closest to the fountain machine. Christine came over and slapped the order in the open window to the kitchen. Turning around, she saw Brock, and her face lit up.

"Brock, honey, I didn't expect to see you here. Are you hungry? Do you want something?"

"Sure, Mom. Just a burger, please. But I am here to tell you I am ready. I know where I'm going." Brock just realized that through all of his planning and excitement for the new adventure, that he would be leaving his mom behind. Christine could see the sadness in his eyes and came around to the front of the counter to give him another hug.

"Honey I am so glad you can finally leave. I don't want you to worry about me or anything else here, okay? This is what you need," she said while still holding him tight.

"Now, let me fill you up so you can get a good night's sleep before you travel." She was walking back around and scribbling his order on her pad. She put it on the window for the kitchen to grab and then turned around and filled him a drink. "So, tell me. Where did you decide to go?" she asked in a happy tone.

Joining her positive attitude, Brock answered happily. "I am going to Vegas! I already have a couple of places in mind to live, and I have a cheap hotel in the meantime to hold me over, and I figured there are going to be plenty of jobs there that I can learn and get really good at..." Brock took a breath, realizing he just spewed all this out in one go.

Christine chuckled and grinned from ear to ear. "That's so awesome, Brock! When do you leave?"

"First thing tomorrow. There's only one bus a day that goes out of town, and I will be on it. I already have my ticket!"

"Order's up!" came from behind Christine. Snapping back to reality and remembering she was working, she spun around, grabbed the plates, and walked over to the corner table.

Brock spent another hour or so at the diner, talking to his mom and imagining what it would be like when he arrived in Vegas. He barely slept that night and was eager to leave the next morning. Hoping to see his mom one more time, he leapt from his bed and walked out into the kitchen area.

"Mom, are you home?" No one answered. Looking down at the round table, he saw a note.

Brock, I'm sorry I couldn't be here to say goodbye this morning but I want you to know that I am so proud of you and I love you very much.

You are going to do amazing things in Vegas. All my love, Mom.

    Sliding the note into his backpack and looking around the place one more time, he grabbed his bags and walked out the door—leaving his key behind.

Part 3
A Whole New World

It wouldn't be accurate to say that Brock was sheltered as a kid growing up. He had access to the internet, he knew about other places he could go, and the TV was always highlighting the fun and exciting opportunities life had to offer. But in reality, those images and alluring temptations always hid the truth.

It was about a nine-hour bus ride to get to Vegas. Leaving behind his mom and the "living landfill," as he sometimes called it, Brock arrived with flashing lights to greet him. It was now 5 p.m., and the Vegas strip was buzzing!

Everywhere Brock looked there were people walking around, laughing and having a good time. The streets were full of cars and limos, and the lights from every hotel and casino were dancing before his eyes. Brock, now off the bus with his luggage, smiled and took it all in. His excitement to begin this new journey was nothing but adrenaline right now. Brock couldn't wait to get himself moving and living in this wild city.

Walking up the concrete ramp that led to the hotel he was going to be staying in, Brock walked through the revolving doors to be greeted again by thousands of flashing lights. Attractive ladies were promoting shows just beyond the main entrance. Slot machines and card tables were in a pit lower down, and off to his right stood some restaurants. The hotel check-in was further down on the left, so that is where Brock went.

After a short wait, he was finally able to get himself to a desk where a very attractive, young woman, about Brock's age, stood waiting to help him.

"Welcome to the Luxor, my name is Rachel, how are you today?" she said with a glowing smile.

Brock was a little flustered. The way he was acting made it look like he'd never even seen a female before, never mind talked to one.

"You're good!" he said randomly. "I mean, I'm good! You're good too...probably. No, you are. I'm sure." Brock stopped talking and replaced words with a very deep shade of red.

Rachel chuckled and smiled at Brock like you would at a puppy that sneezed for the first time.

"Do you have a reservation with us? Can I see your ID and credit card?"

Brock simply kept his mouth shut this time and focused on getting his cards to give to her.

Rachel began looking up his information, and Brock could do nothing more than just admire her. Her long, brown hair neatly tied behind her, her eyes a glowing blue color. Brock was in love.

"I just got here," Brock said, finally.

"Yes, welcome to the Luxor, Brock."

"No, sorry, I mean to Vegas. I decided to move here. This is my first time in Vegas."

"Oh, I see. What made you decide to move to Vegas, especially if you've never been here before?"

"It's sort of a long story, but I needed to leave. There was nothing for me back home."

"Well, I hope you find what you're looking for here, Brock. You are all checked in. Your room is 322, and the elevator you need is the East Elevator which is down here on your right. I hope you enjoy your stay."

"Thank you, Rachel. It was nice to meet you."

"Likewise, Brock. Welcome to Vegas." With both of them smiling at each other, Brock grabbed his luggage and headed to his elevator and finally his room. Of course, he did look back at the check-in desk one more time to see if she was watching...she was, and she smiled.

Brock finally made it to his room and inside was everything he hoped for. A king size bed, a view of the pool below and, of course, the Las Vegas Strip. The room itself wasn't anything to brag about, but Brock didn't care. It was nicer than anything he had back home. Leaving his bags by the wall, Brock flopped onto the bed and took in a few breaths of relief.

"I made it," he whispered.

A few seconds later, the phone in his room rang. Puzzled, Brock got up and gingerly answered. "Hello?"

"Brock, this is Rachel at the front desk. I just wanted to make sure you got to your room and everything looked satisfactory for you."

"Wow, umm, yes this is great. Thanks, Rachel."

"Also, I was wondering...I don't usually do this, but I get off at

7...would you like to meet me down here and we can get some food? I'd love to hear more about why you moved here."

"Umm, I, you do...Yes, you would. I would, I would...what I mean is...I would love that. I will see you around 7 downstairs."

"Okay, see you then," she said, chuckling as she hung up."

Brock looked at the clock. It was already 5:30. Brock grabbed his bags and looked for a nicer shirt to wear, and then realized he should probably shower too.

By 7:05, Brock was in the lobby, smelling much nicer and looking a little more put together. Rachel soon came out and off they went out the front door of the hotel.

"So where should we go?" Rachel asked.

"I have literally no idea..." Brock said.

49

"Don't worry, I'm just teasing. I know a great place not far from here." Rachel slid her hand onto Brock's arm, and they walked quite happily, talking about anything and everything—and eventually all about Brock's past life.

Part 4
Work, Work, Work

"No, Mom, I'm doing okay. I'm figuring things out, I promise," Brock said as he paced in his hotel room. "It's only been four days, but I think I found a place to live. I just need to get the job part nailed down, and I'll be fine. Look, Mom, someone is knocking at my door, I need to go...Yes, I love you too...I will, bye."

Brock hung up the phone and threw it on the bed. Flopping down, he buried his face into the cotton covered pillow. Brock had lied. There was no one at his door, and he didn't have a place figured out to live, and the job...that was not a topic he wanted to discuss.

Every apartment Brock went to visit was either in a horrible part of town or didn't offer something that he could afford. All of his viewings were done and he was no closer to landing on his feet. Thankfully, Rachel was able to extend his hotel room for a few more nights at a very low rate as a favor to the new friend she had made.

Brock decided it was time he left his room. It was after 10 a.m. already, and he needed time to stretch his legs, think, and get some air. Leaving the hotel, he stepped out into the hot sun where bodies were buzzing all around him. The "fish out of water" feeling was overwhelming, but it didn't stop him.

Without having a real direction, Brock just started walking. His initial thought was just to see what hotels were close by and apply at one of those. However, it wasn't that simple. Being surrounded by so many casinos, it was hard to figure out how to get himself hooked up to an application process, or even speak to the right person.

There was one thing though...Brock remembered seeing a billboard in the distance from his hotel room about a company that might be in his wheelhouse. Crossing over I-15, Brock could soon see the building for RSD—Refrigeration

Supplies Distributor. Brock assumed the attitude that not trying was the worst thing, and all they could do was say no.

Finally approaching the building, he was greeted by a nice-looking parking lot and an array of windows that mirrored the Luxor. This was much nicer than anything back home, and Brock felt intimidated immediately. But it was now or never. He needed work no matter what, and this might be the one thing he could do without needing much training.

Approaching the door, he took a deep breath and stepped into the nice air-conditioned room. Music could be heard from the ceiling ever so slightly, a few plants surrounded the desk area to create a welcoming ambiance, and the sitting area looked comfortable and relaxing. This was literally the opposite of what Brock was used to—he was liking this already.

"Can I help you? Are you lost?" came a soft voice from behind the desk.

Brock walked forward and approached the woman sitting at the desk. She was at a computer with a headset and, filing cabinets sat tall behind her.

"Hi, my name is Brock, Brock Miles. I was hoping to get an application? I just got into Vegas a few days ago, and I am looking to make this my home."

"Oh, well welcome, Mr. Miles. Our applications are accepted online, through a resume. Do you have any experience?"

"Well, in my hometown I worked in a factory setting for years. I am certainly used to the work, and I was good at it too. They ended up laying off a lot of people, so I decided it was time for a change."

"Well, okay. I'll tell you what. Take this card, it has my number on it, my name is Sally. If you need any help while you're getting that all together, you just let me know, okay? We do have positions that need to be filled so get it in as soon as you can and my boss will be able to take a look."

"That sounds great. Could you put the website I should go to on the card?"

"No need. Here, this is the information we need, the website, all the details to get it done right the first time are on here." Smiling, she handed Brock a piece of paper with a list of instructions filling about half of the page.

"Thank you so much, Sally, I will get on this right away."

"Take care..."

And with that, Brock was out the door and headed back to his hotel room. As he walked, he glanced over some of the prerequisites. Brock soon realized he was going to need some help. With his phone out, he sent a quick text message to Rachel.

Rachel. Can you help me after your shift? I have an application to fill out, but I need help completing it. Can you bring your laptop?

By the time Brock got back to his room, he had checked his phone about ten times to see if he missed her reply. But it wasn't until about 1 p.m. that she finally replied.

Sorry, Brock, I'm not working today. But if you want, you could come over?

That would be amazing. Where do you live?

Rachel texted the address and Brock soon grabbed a taxi that was lying in wait for the tourists. After about fifteen minutes, he was at her door.

The building was nice. Sand-colored like most of the buildings in the area, but the overall appearance was very inviting. Brock hadn't seen this on his list.

Rachel's door was bright blue, a welcome mat sat on the floor, and a cactus plant sat next to the wall that jutted out. Knocking a few times, it wasn't long before a bubbly Rachel answered, followed by a nosy dog.

"Don't mind him, he won't bite. Come on in, Brock."

"Thanks, Rachel, this is definitely a life-saver. I need this job so bad."

"Don't mention it. Sit anywhere you like, I'll grab my laptop."

With the dog promptly following Brock, sniffing every inch possible, Brock took a seat on the edge of the plush couch and instantly felt relaxed. Now it was just a matter of figuring out how to get the resume he didn't have, done promptly.

Part 5
A Year Later

"Hi, Mom..." Brock stood in the doorway of the diner. Spinning around, his mom about dropped the empty plates she was bussing from a nearby table. Setting them down on the counter, she ran over to her baby boy.

"Brock! You made it home!" She hugged him tight and didn't want to let go. "My goodness, look at you. You look amazing!"

Standing back, she examined him like any mother would and was beaming with delight at how well dressed he was.

"Come in. Sit, sit. I am due for a break anyway. I want to hear everything..."

For the next thirty to forty minutes, Brock regaled his mother all about Rachel and his job which was amazing. Brock had already moved up to a managerial level due to his knowledge and fast-paced work ethic.

His apartment was in a nice part of town, just a street away from Rachel, who he wasn't yet dating, but hoped to be very soon.

"Mom, I can't begin to tell you how much my life has turned around. At first, I thought I was going to disappoint you and come home broke and have nothing to show for it. But now I have a great job, a decent place to stay, and new friends. You will have to come visit!"

"Brock, that's so wonderful. I am so proud of you. But listen, honey, I really do need to get back to work. How about I meet you back at the house and we can talk more there?"

"Sure thing, Mom, I will see you at home."

A few hours passed by the time Brock's mom walked in the door. She had a few bags with groceries and set them down on the kitchen table.

Brock came in and gave her a hug and a kiss on the cheek.

"Let me help, Mom, you go sit down."

"I'm sorry. I was supposed to be meeting my son here, who are you?" she said with a chuckle.

"Rachel has had a good effect on me. I do my own laundry now too..." Brock stuck out his tongue to be playful.

While putting groceries in cupboards and in the pantry, his mom sat on the couch in the adjacent living room.

"Honey, those can wait, come sit down, there is something I need to talk to you about."

"Okay, sure. What is it, Mom?" Brock asked with an inkling of concern.

"Brock, there's no easy way for me to tell you this, so I'm just going to say it." She took his hand and gripped it tight. "Honey I have cancer. I was diagnosed not long after you left. I..."

Brock cut her off. He let go of her hand and stood up, trying to absorb this dramatic news.

"When were you going to tell me? What kind of cancer? Are you being helped? Why am I just finding out now?!" Brock was both angry and in shock. He didn't know what to do.

Sitting back down, she hugged him as if it were he that just got the news.

"The cancer is small right now, but it's spreading. The doctors here, they can't help me, and I certainly can't afford a fancy hospital."

"I took your money! I took your money! You can have every penny I have. I will come home, I will take care of you, Mom."

"You will do no such thing!" she said in a stern voice as if Brock just broke a window. Brock immediately stopped. His attention was fully hers. "You have done so well for yourself, Brocky... I don't know how much time I have left, but I sure won't let you spend it by throwing everything away."

"Then come with me. I have a spare room. I can take care of you in Vegas. You don't need the house, sell it. Come live with me. I will not leave you here, alone, with no one to help you."

Embracing again, Brock felt he had won that argument.

"On one condition, Brock."

"Name it," Brock said in angst.

"If I come to live with you, you are NOT allowed to stop living your new life just because I am there. You understand me?"

"Mom...you are my life. Come on, let's figure out what we can pack."

Brock and his mom spent the rest of the evening packing as many suitcases as they could carry between them. It wasn't a great deal, but deep down they both knew it wouldn't matter.

The next day, arrangements were made to have the house appraised and then put on the market for immediate sale. Both Brock and his mom were soon headed to Vegas so she could live out her remaining days with the only family she had left.

Part 6
This Was It

The heat was unbearable. Midday and not a cloud in the sky. Still, it wouldn't be the worst thing ever. Brock, on his break at work, was admiring the view while sipping on an ice cold water. Just as he was about to go back in, his boss, the head manager appeared from around the corner.

"Ah, Brock, I'm glad I found you."

"What do you need, sir? I was just on my back in."

"Yeah look, hold on for a second. I want to talk to you. Look...I heard about your mom." Brock put down his water and sat down on the nearby bench. "I know. I know. You were keeping it to yourself, but talk doesn't take long to get around in here, we are a tight group."

"Yeah, I guess I should have known it would get out sooner or later."

"Brock you've been doing some great work for us here, but you haven't taken any time off at all. I want you to take a week. Go be with your mom. It's time with people that you will never get back."

"I appreciate that, Mr. Seems, but I can't afford a whole week off. I could maybe do..."

Mr. Seems interrupted him. "Don't worry about your paycheck. We are taking care of that. All I want you to do is think about all the different experiences you want to have with your mother before those chances are gone. And that starts now...go home!" Mr. Seems finished with a smile and stuck out his hand.

Brock looked up at him, smiled back, took his hand, and stood up. "Thanks, Mr. Seems. I really appreciate it."

"You're welcome, kid. See you in a week."

About thirty minutes later, and Brock was back home putting his key into the lock. Once inside, he heard laughing and chatter coming from the living room. Confused, Brock popped his head around the corner to see what was going on.

"Brock, hey you're home early?!" Rachel was sitting with Brock's mom, and they must have been having a good time too.

"Doing a little day drinking...are we?" Brock said with his mothers' tone.

"Busted! You caught me!" said his mom with her arms up. "I wasn't expecting to see you so soon, dear."

"Yeah, my boss, he just walked up to me today and told me to take a week off so I could spend more time with you."

"What a great boss! Come here, give your mother a hug."

Brock went over to the couch and plopped next to his mother and gave her a good squeeze. The apartment was as nice as Brock told his mom. The couches were leather, the TV was large, and the finishings were all high-end.

The rest of the week they spent a lot of time together, and Rachel joined in whenever her time allowed. They walked the strip and took in all the lights. Taking frequent breaks as his mom was getting weaker, they were able to talk about the old days and what life was like growing up. In between shows and meals out, they discussed the future and what might happen for Brock and Rachel.

On Brock's last day off, he took both his mom and Rachel to the Grand Canyon for a tour. Rachel had been before, but she never missed an opportunity to enjoy its magnificence.

By this time, however, Brock's mom was really taking a turn for the worse. She could barely stand, and as stubborn as she was, Brock knew it was nearly time. So he decided it was now that he needed to take the next step.

"Rachel..." he said as he got down on one knee. "I knew from the minute I met you at the Luxor that there was something special about you. I didn't know what it was at the time, but over the past year, I have come to know a sweet, and special lady who cares about everyone and everything in her life. You make me feel complete. So now I want to make your life complete too... Will you by bride? Will you marry me?"

By this time, Rachel was basically weeping, and the entire crowd around them had stopped to focus in.

"Yes! Of course!" Rachel flew into his arms as they hugged and kissed. And Brock's mom let out the loudest cheer she could muster. Everyone around cheered and applauded the happy couple...nothing could ruin this moment. Except of course, cancer.

Brock's mom, in all her excitement, began coughing and gasping. Brock yelled out for someone to call 911. Thankfully, there was a nurse nearby and she helped Brock's mom get comfortable enough to where she wasn't coughing so much, but her pulse was weak.

The hospital's air-care showed up and were able to take Brock's mom to the hospital. Brock and Rachel took off from the Grand Canyon as fast as they could, racing to the hospital themselves. It took a long time to get out of the Canyon, but they made every second count. Upon arrival, they figured out where she was and got to her bedside as fast as they could. Before even getting through her door, they were stopped.

"Are you her son?" a doctor asked as they rushed in with labored breath.

"Yes, my name is Brock, this is Rachel, my fiancé," he said, squeezing her hand tightly.

"Son, I don't know how much you know, but this cancer is terminal. We can keep her comfortable, but there isn't much we can do. I'm honestly surprised she's made it this long. We did an x-ray immediately upon her arrival, and I'm afraid it's just too much. Her body is shutting down."

"It's okay, Doctor. I already know. I knew this day was coming, I...we just didn't know how much time was left. I guess I just hoped it would be longer. Can I see her?"

"She's sedated for now, and on a breathing tube so she doesn't have to work hard, but yes you can."

Brock and Rachel slowly walked through the door. This was it.

Part 7
A New Future

Creaking wood of an old pew. The scent of freshly picked tulips. The faces of so few, but so few faces that had full hearts. This was everything that Brock saw.

He stood up from the first row. The casket to his left, closed and sealed. Stepping up to stand above the few that were there, he poised himself, looked Rachel in the eye, and then looked out to the faces watching.

"My mother, she was an example to me and many others. She may not have known this, but her life, the way in which she lived taught me so much more than I could have realized. I just wish I had realized sooner.

"She had little but gave everything. In her times of need, she made do with what she had and didn't complain. She had to work all the time, and yet still made sure I was taken care of.

"As much as I will miss her, I also recognize how much of her is within me. I can be like her. I can show kindness to the stranger. I can be a helping hand where there is none. I can show the world what it means to be a 'Mills.'

"That is why, with the money received from her home sale, and all other possessions, that instead of keeping the money for myself, I am starting a new fund that will help those with cancer right here in this community. It won't be much at first, but once I gain some ground from my new home community—it will thrive.

"I don't know how to stop cancer. But I do know, thanks to my mother, how to spread love and kindness to everyone I meet." Brock looked over at the casket. A tear rolled down his right cheek.

"Mom. Wherever you are, I need you to know that you are loved and missed deeply. But it's your turn to rest." Brock stepped down and sat back in his pew. Rachel, wrapping her arm around him, whispered in his ear.

Many months passed after this day, and Las Vegas hadn't changed much. Brock was hard at work, and Rachel eventually moved in with him. Wedding plans were coming along nicely and things were looking up for Brock and Rachel. Little did Brock know, the kind of impact his words would have at his mother's funeral.

That evening, around 6 p.m., Brock received a phone call while he and Rachel were eating their leftovers for dinner.

"Yes, hello, is this Brock—Brock Mills?"

"It is...who is calling please?" Brock looked confused as the caller ID was blocked.

"Mr. Mills, my name is Matthew Henderson. A name that you have probably never heard before. But I heard about you, and more importantly, I heard about what you said at your mother's funeral."

"Okay, go on..." said Brock, a little un-nerved.

"Mr. Mills, I would like to make sure your new cause gets the funding it so desperately needs..."

Mr. Henderson kept talking, and as he did, Brock slowly sat down as if he had seen a ghost and needed to not pass out. As soon as their conversation ended, he put down the phone and looked at Rachel, who herself was very lost.

"Who was that? Why do you look so pale?"

"You're not going to believe what just happened..." Brock chuckled a little, still trying to believe the news himself.

"There are still some details to figure out, but that was a Mr. Henderson. He is a very wealthy casino owner right here in Vegas. He wants to be the financial backer to the cancer fund that I started. He has a whole team of people ready to help with marketing and branding...the whole works."

"What?!" said Rachel, rather loudly.

Laughing, Brock continued. "He...he told me not to worry about going back to work on Monday—he will be paying my new salary going forward. And he will call me on Friday with more details."

Brock and Rachel were beside themselves. They didn't know what to think other than to realize that life can be surprising.

Eventually, Brock and Rachel did get married, and they moved out of the apartment and into a new home built just for them. His new charitable foundation was being backed with more money than he knew what to do with, and folks from all around were now receiving the money to fight cancer when there was none before.

It didn't take Brock long to realize that sometimes things happen for a reason. Even when the worst of life is in front of you, it doesn't mean that in the future you can't find something to hold onto.

Brock's future was very bright indeed.

THE END

Security Cop Story 1

Part 1
Roger's Intro

Sitting on his couch with the TV on, Roger dipped his hand back into the large bag of chips sitting between his legs and poured his catch into his mouth.

It was summertime and hot outside. Roger had no intentions of going anywhere, anytime soon. And with his favorite show on all day, COPS, he relaxed and glued himself to the screen.

Roger lived in a somewhat small apartment that initially was for him, and only him. Being twenty-four years old, he had zero ambitions of doing anything spectacular and planned on being a bachelor for as long as he could.

The building itself held four apartments. When entering through the main door, a split-level landing split the stairs for both apartments on the bottom and top.

The layout was the same in all the apartments except for one significant difference...Roger had a fireplace, and no else did. Roger thought this would be beneficial for bringing home the ladies and using the fireplace as a beautiful scenic background; If only he could get some "ladies" to come back with him to use the space as he had hoped.

Roger's place was the bottom right apartment. Opposite him were a bunch of "kids" that he knew did drugs on a regular basis, but he didn't mind so much as they were quiet and kept to themselves. Above them was a single guy in his forties, living alone, and even more modest still. And directly above Roger, lived a young, vibrant lesbian couple. They, however, couldn't care less about who heard what and when. Roger was on speaking terms with them, but I wouldn't say they were friends.

Inside Roger's apartment, you were immediately sent to the open living and dining area. The kitchen was next to the dining area if you could even call it a kitchen. In front of the kitchen was the hallway that led to a bathroom, and two bedrooms. The smallest of bedrooms was more like a glamorous closet due to its petite size.

Roger lived merely, mainly because he didn't care about filling the space with "stuff," other than the technology he liked. His TV wasn't the latest and greatest, but he did string up a 5.1 Surround Sound with the speakers mounted on the wall.

The couch was an older, itchy material with no specific pattern on it; certainly, something from a garage sale or discount store. The carpet was red and cheap, but he didn't mind, and the kitchen was extremely limited on cabinets, but it did have a dishwasher, which was rare. Because of the dishwasher and brick fireplace, his rent was higher.

Roger delivered bread. This meant he was up very early and off work before everyone else. He loved the job though because he never had to work weekends and because of the early starts, his pay was pretty high. Rent wasn't a problem and that left money for other things like his surround sound.

It just so happened that while Roger was eating his chips and watching reruns of COPS, he got a text from a friend of his.

Roger, you need to come out tonight, I know this girl who is into you.

Roger was a little puzzled by the text as he had no idea who it could be. His buddy, Clive, aka "Stix" was always trying to set Roger up with someone, and they always failed, but hey, what else was Roger going to do on a dreary Sunday. He fired back a message.

Hey, Stix. I work in the morning, so maybe we can meet for dinner or something? I'll be hitting the sack early tonight.

Instantly Clive replied. *Yeah sure, that was the plan. Meet us over at Room 83 Bar & Grill. 6 p.m., don't be late!*

Sounds good Stix, see you there.

Part 2
Lisa and Roger

When Roger sat down at the table, Stix and his girlfriend were already there, along with the mystery woman. Roger was blown away and immediately intimidated by how gorgeous she looked. Roger was immediately nervous and unable to think correctly.

The beautiful woman he was about to sit next to was a knock-out. Her blonde hair dropped to her shoulders, her smile drew him in as he examined the rest of her. She wore a spaghetti strap top that clung to her every curve. It was black, and from what he could tell, she was not wearing a bra. Her jeans were dark blue and clung to her, and her feet were covered by black boots with a small heel.

Roger sat next to her and smiled. "You're Roger. I mean, I'm Roger, it's hot too, oh my goodness...it's great to meet you." Roger could have stopped traffic. His face was burning red. He looked away, feeling like an idiot, grabbed his water, and sipped it to try and clear his throat.

Luckily for Roger, this lovely, young lady was not put off by his fumbling words. "I'm Lisa. But if you need to call me Roger, I will consider it." She laughed and put her hand on his shoulder for a brief moment. That was it. He was hooked. Roger did not care what he had to do, Lisa was going to be his girl at some point.

Surprisingly, the night went quite smooth from that point on. The four of them dined and laughed and told stories about each other. Roger learned that Lisa was twenty-seven years old and working on becoming a pharmacist. Roger was quite impressed with Lisa and the type of person she was. Even though the idea of a relationship was not his goal, he was suddenly considering the idea of one.

After the meal was done, and the conversations exhausted, Roger looked at his phone and saw it was 8:30 p.m. Apologizing, he excused himself due to his early morning schedule, but before leaving, he made sure to get Lisa's number and vice versa.

Over the next few months, Roger changed. He started caring about how his dinky apartment looked, and how he looked. The friendship that was built between Roger and Lisa was special and about to change into something more significant, or at least he hoped.

Summer turned to fall, and then to winter, and by now, Lisa had moved in. The spare room did become a closet space, mainly for Lisa and her shoes and clothes as there was not enough room in the main bedroom.

The two of them were very happy together and became inseparable. It didn't matter where Roger and Lisa went or what they did, as long as they did it together, it was the most fun and best time of their lives. Roger was on cloud nine, but just like gravity, what goes up, must come down—and it came down hard.

Part 3
The Fall

It had been a year and three months that Lisa and Roger had been officially dating and living together. Things between them had been going amazing. Roger never thought he would see this day, and especially with someone so amazing as Lisa.

When Lisa came home on Friday, she did so with a beaming smile on her face. It was the end of the fall semester, and Lisa could barely hold her excitement. Roger was standing in the kitchen unwrapping a pizza to cook.

"Put the pizza back, Roger. We are going out tonight!" she said with a giddy, childlike posture.

"Okay, umm, where are we going? What happened today?" Roger was also smiling, but only because it seemed like the correct response. He was clueless as to what was happening.

"Roger!" she said almost disappointingly. "I just got my certification. I am a bona fide Pharmacist!"

"Oh my gosh, that's great!" Roger finally connected the dots and ran to her and kissed her all over.

The two of them got dressed up and went out to eat to celebrate her success. Roger couldn't keep his eyes off her. She wore a new and very revealing red dress. She looked irresistible, and Roger wanted to skip the main course and go straight for dessert!

Their night was filled with pictures, tasty food, drinks, dancing, and memories to last a lifetime. Roger was the happiest guy in the world, and nothing could break that.

Lisa, on the other hand, although thrilled about her new title, which meant a raise and more perks to the job, was concerned about their relationship. It was perfect, and that was the problem. In Lisa's mind, it was so perfect that moving it in a new direction scared her but not because she didn't want more; instead it was Roger. Roger was content with his role with the bread delivery company and had no plans of changing. The apartment was okay, but the walls were caving in on her, and she wanted a nicer place.

Over time, the feelings she had became more evident in their relationship, and what was once a place full of life, was now becoming a college dorm room.

And then one day, it happened. It was two weeks before Roger's birthday. He ended his route early because some of his usual drop off points didn't need anything new on that particular day. It happened every so often, and Roger loved it as it meant more time not working.

As Roger went down the steps, it was quiet. Putting his key in the door, he suddenly paused. Roger could hear another man's voice and moaning coming from Lisa. In a panic, and with the feeling he was going to throw up, he slowly unlocked the door and walked in.

The once muffled sounds now became very clear, and even though he didn't want to believe it, he could not dismiss what he heard from his bedroom.

"Oh my god, yeah, just like that!"

Roger couldn't believe what he was hearing coming out of Lisa's mouth. He thought their sex life was good, but she never talked to him in that way. Now he had to figure out how to do this.

"Do I just bust in? Do I quietly open the door and wait to be noticed?" he mumbled to himself as he slowly walked down the hall to the door.

Roger's hand was reaching for the round, bronze handle and was shaking the entire time. He decided that busting in was his best bet. Once he had the handle firmly in his grasp, he took a deep breath and plowed the door open.

The bed was the first thing you would see in the bedroom. The dresser was off to the right, and the closet was to the left. The room was long, but not very deep. As soon as Roger stepped in, Lisa, who was on her hands and knees, screamed and tried to stand up and cover herself out of shame.

The guy who was just giving her a good time froze like a deer in headlights.

"I don't know who you are, but you better get the hell out right now, or I am going to make you wish you were never born!" Roger had no idea he could become this angry, but his rage was just beginning.

The man behind his girlfriend grabbed his clothes and bolted out of the bedroom and then the apartment. Assumingly he would dress in the stairway, but Roger did not give a damn.

Lisa was trying to speak but was inaudible because of her tears and nervous shaking. She could see how mad Roger was, and she didn't know what to do. Roger looked her in the eye, and without speaking, turned and walked into the living room.

A minute later, a somewhat dressed Lisa appeared and tried to start talking, but was interrupted.

"I'm going to take a drive. You have until I get back to get your crap and get the hell out of my apartment. You no longer live here, and we are no longer together. And to think I was going to propose..." He started talking to himself at this point, but Lisa could still hear him. Gut wrenched, she cried even more as she realized what she had just done.

"I can't believe I bought the stupid ring. What was I thinking..." He stopped mumbling and walked toward the door, walking past Lisa without making eye contact and just walked out.

Lisa stood frozen for a moment. This all happened so quickly, and her head couldn't process anything right now. In shock, Lisa turned and went to the bedroom and finished getting dressed. She grabbed a bag and filled it with as much of her clothing as she could and took it to her car. Repeating this process, with laundry baskets and whatever else she could use to carry her belongings, she filled her car to the brim.

By the time Roger came home, Lisa was gone as requested. No note. Just an empty apartment that was full of misery and pain. This changed Roger, and like flicking a light switch, he suddenly felt determined to change things. His primary goal was to make her realize what she just threw away. Roger wanted Lisa to feel as bad as possible, and in his mind, changing his life was the best way to do it.

Considering his birthday was two weeks away, turning twenty-eight was a wake-up call.

"Can I deliver bread forever? Probably not. I need to do something big. And I think I know what it is..."

Roger was infatuated with the show COPS, and so, why not become one? Power, authority, control, there wasn't much else he would need to make Lisa feel stupid. So that was his new plan, and he began figuring out the pieces the very next day.

Part 4
When a Plan Doesn't Come Together

Roger isolated the event that recently occurred and poured his energy into his new pursuit. Every minute he wasn't delivering bread, he spent researching what he needed to join the Police Department. So far, he knew he needed his degree which, although not in criminal justice, he hoped they would overlook. Roger knew there would be a written test of some kind, a physical, and also a psych evaluation.

There was a lot to plan for, and some changes that needed to be made. After calling the police station, he learned that his degree would be acceptable, but he needed to take a few extra classes to qualify through the initial application process.

Over the next six months, Roger transformed himself from an "average Joe," to a ripped Roger! Not only was Roger in great physical shape, but he was also blazing through his classes at the local community college. Roger just needed three, and two of those Roger could do online. It wasn't long before he was filing his paper application with confidence he'd never had.

Weeks went by after Roger's application went in. Roger was growing impatient and was becoming untangled. Every time he felt frustrated, regardless of where he was, his mind went back to him putting his key in the door and hearing...them.

While coming home from work one day, Roger stopped to get gas and noticed a man there wearing a security uniform. Approaching him, he inquired about what he did and how he could apply. It wasn't long before Roger was back at home applying online for that job also.

"This is just temporary," he told himself, as he knew it wouldn't be anything close to the real thing, but Roger was desperate to get started somehow. The pay was less than what he made now, but he managed to save enough to cover the difference, for about a year or so. "Plenty of time," he told himself.

A few days later, he was being interviewed and was hired on the spot for a position as a Security Officer. A perk for Roger was that they agreed to bump his pay after his sixty-day evaluation to a more than reasonable amount, considering his financial situation if he didn't earn enough. This was also because of his criminal justice classes, everything he had been doing was pointing toward success.

Roger quit his bread delivery job right after his paycheck came in, and began orientation with "Security Plus." It wasn't long before Roger was shadowing other officers and learning the ropes first hand.

One day after shadowing, Roger got a phone call from the Police Department. They wanted to set up the psych evaluation for Monday next week. He wasn't working that day, so Roger was all for it.

When the day arrived, Roger was calm, and collected; or at least he thought he was. The questioning was going fine right up until the point of relationships. Roger froze. His mind went numb as he sifted through the replays of that painful day. Suddenly, his interviewer turned into a counselor. Roger exploded with emotion and unraveled the event that took place in his apartment. His interviewer, an older woman with small, square glasses, made plenty of notes as she looked at Roger over the top of the rims.

Then, the interview ended. Roger was told to wait for a letter in the mail on the results and instructions for the next steps if he qualified to continue. Until that time, Roger kept a close eye on his mailbox. All the mailboxes were located on the bottom floor of the apartment building between his apartment, and the drug addicts next door.
Roger worked and waited, worked and waited. It took three

weeks in total for the letter to arrive, and by that time he was very well adjusted to his new role. Roger was set up at multiple accounts that the security company monitored and was showing great initiative with his work, including making suggestions and helping others become better at their job.

Roger's sixty-day review proved to be excellent. He not only got his raise but was also promoted to a manager level. It was unusual for someone to rise in the ranks that quickly, but Roger was showing tremendous efforts and earned his new role.

When the letter did arrive, he sat down on his couch, and slowly opened the letter. After only mere seconds the letter, almost in slow motion, dropped to the carpet below and Roger rested back in his seat silently, but in pain. His application process with the Police Department was over. He was denied due to an "unstable emotional state."

Roger never did come to terms with what happened or took the appropriate time to grieve and process the situation. Roger had been in relationships before, but this was the first time he felt something real; it just turns out she didn't feel the same.

Roger asked for some personal time off work, which he was granted. During this time, he decided enough was enough and that he had to move on. He also needed to move out.

He found a smaller, one-bedroom apartment without the fireplace or any other unique amenities, and loaded up what he needed and tossed the rest. During his time in the new apartment, he managed to suppress his anger and control it. Roger was becoming healthier now also in his head, just as he was with his physical fitness.

Roger was a calmer, happier guy. And a new work assignment was waiting for him when he got back to work; something about a Warehouse construction site.

The End

SECURITY COP STORY 2

PART 1
ROGER'S ON DUTY

The room was very silent and extremely dark, all except for the alarm clock that faced Roger on his nightstand. It was a good thing alarm clocks were machines because this one would have felt sorry for what it was about to do.

It was 01:59, and any second now, it was about to blast a cruel alarm to wake Roger up for his shift. You see, Roger works twelve-hour shifts from 3:00 a.m. to 3:00 p.m., three days a week. And this morning, it was the last of his three work days in a row.

Sure enough, as 2:00 a.m. struck, the alarm clock blared an ear piercing alarm which startled Roger and shook him awake. With fast reflexes (at least for 2:00 a.m.), he hit the snooze button to shut up the alarm.

At least Roger lived alone. There was a time when his girlfriend lived with him, but due to her abrupt departure after cheating on him, this set up was easier to handle.

Being twenty-nine, and in somewhat decent shape, he started to hate the work that he did. Roger had goals, dreams, aspirations of becoming something that Lisa (his ex-girlfriend) could be proud of. But like usual, something always got in the way.

Every morning as he dressed for work, he thought about what he really wanted to be, and then was reminded of her—of Lisa. As soon as she got her promotion at the pharmacy, he could feel her looking down on him. Even though it was never said out loud, he could tell she wanted him to become something more significant.

With his black pressed pants, blue shirt, clip-on tie, and flashlight all ready, he looked himself over in the mirror one more time and then grabbed his pre-made breakfast (or was it lunch?) and headed out the door.

At least for Roger, the commute wasn't that bad. The only things he typically encountered at 2:30 a.m. were Semi's usually on long hauls, and pulled over vehicles for most likely drinking and driving.

When he first began this work, he used to count how many cop cars Roger saw on the interstate and streets to his work, and then count how many cars he saw swerving before being caught. If the cop cars outnumbered the swerving vehicles, the cops would win. If it was the other way around, he shook his head and muttered how he could do better.

After all, that was his dream. To be a city cop working his beat. He didn't care when in the twenty-four hours he could do it, he just badly wanted to do it. Roger had applied once in the past but failed the written exam so in his spare time he studied in hopes of passing his second time around.

But for now, he had to settle for a security position. He would at least give himself hope by reminding himself that at least he still wore some sort of uniform. Even if he did hate it deep down.

His commute only took about twenty minutes, and it was a smooth drive getting there. There, being old warehouses that were set for reconstruction. These particular buildings were going to be turned into apartments on top, and stores and bars or restaurants on the bottom.

Right now, there wasn't much of anything happening, but they had been bought, and the new owner didn't want anyone messing with his buildings. The building Roger looked after for twelve painstaking hours was four stories tall and currently sat with construction equipment scattered all around the outside, with lumber and other materials protected from the elements inside.

The best part about the job, though, was the view. Roger wasn't precisely a sentimental guy, but something about seeing the sun come up warmed his soul—it gave him hope. Plus, the best view was from the top floor looking out over the river.

Back in the day, these buildings were busy factories, and the river was a favorite import/export channel, along with the close by railways. But now they would become trendy new apartments with amenities and entertainment close by.

Arriving at his post, he parked in his usual spot (not like there was any competition) and went inside to meet the ever-so-lazy Walter. Walter was standing there, clipboard and radio in hand, ready to pass off to Roger and call it a night. His shirt, half untucked and his pants filthy, he smiled and greeted Roger.

"Always early, always eager...you need to find a new hobby, Roger," he said, laughing at his own joke.

Which, of course, Roger didn't find amusing the time, or the countless other times he heard that from Walter.

"Anything happen on your shift I should know about, Walter?" he said with an assumed answer of, no.

"I think I scared away a raccoon? Goodnight, Roger, try not to keep all the excitement to yourself, okay?" And with that, Walter hobbled away.

Walter was much older than Roger, so expecting anything magical from him was asking a lot. This was just retiree work, a small paycheck to waste away at the Casino. But for Roger, this was resume building and performance enhancing work. It may not have looked like much, but he wanted to impress his boss and the owner.

Roger called in that he was starting his shift and that Walter had gone for the day. He checked the battery on the radio, and double-checked that his pen worked on the clipboard. The radio was able to receive the local police band if it came close enough, but it was also for communicating to the owner when he was on site. The owner never showed up until about 9:00 or 10:00 a.m., so Roger always had it set to the police channel.

The clipboard was for him to write down his movements during the shift, anything that might have happened and if he noticed anything "suspicious."

One aspect of the job that he didn't like, but did it just because, was picking up any litter that was found on the worksite. Roger didn't think the work was beneath him but knowing he was basically picking up after the workmen that were there the day before annoyed him, and the fact that Walter didn't help just put the cherry on top. But at least it kept him busy for a little while.

The more Roger learned about what was laying around, especially on the ground floor, the more he realized how valuable some of the stuff here was. There was high-quality lumber scattered throughout, although he couldn't see anyone taking the time to load that up. The item that he knew would be a thief magnet was the copper wiring. Roger found it in large quantities spread throughout the building in strategic locations for the construction crew, but they were exposed.

One particular Friday night, not long after Roger began his shift, he was on the second level and saw someone approach the building from across the street. Roger's "security mode" kicked into high gear because even seeing a human body anywhere around would be strange enough.

The man was wearing ripped blue jeans, and some kind of white t-shirt with stains on the front, or maybe that was artwork on the t-shirt, Roger couldn't tell. The man got closer and then stopped to look inside to see if he would be alone.

Roger, holding his breath waited. As a statue would, he didn't move a muscle, spooking the guy wouldn't allow him to nab a thief!

The assumed thief climbed up the brick wall next to the sidewalk and shimmied his way inside. Sneaking as best he could, he started to look around and soon enough found a stash of copper wire just begging to be stolen. Roger, however, knowing he had gotten into the building had begun to silently move in the thief's direction.

From the top of the stairs, Roger could see the thief attempting to pick up the spool of wire, and also noticed he was struggling. Roger ran down the stairs and yelled at the thief and tackled him to the ground. They fell close to a nearby block of cement bags, and Roger flipped him over and grabbed his handcuffs and slapped them on him.

"What the hell, man?! What are you doing? Get off me!"

Roger smiled. "You're busted, thief. Tonight, you get a jail cell instead of expensive copper."

Roger dialed 911 and explained the situation. It didn't take long for a unit to arrive to assist Roger. Once the officer found Roger, he heard what happened, and that was enough for him.

"Sir, I'm Officer Whittier, and you are being arrested for trespassing on private property and the attempted theft of the copper wire sitting here, do you have any questions?"

Strangely enough, there was only silence from the thief. Officer Whittier read him his rights, exchanged handcuffs with Roger, and hauled the thief away. Pretty soon it was back to dull and quiet, but Roger was on cloud nine. He couldn't wait for his boss to hear about this, and for the owner to know that he saved his job site. Roger was beaming for the rest of his shift.

In the few months that Roger had been posted here, he could

really start to see the place taking shape. The apartment structures were all laid out, and you could begin to see how things might look. Granted, no walls were erected yet, but stepping in through where a door would eventually be, Roger was quickly able to map out the apartment flow. He thought maybe even he wouldn't mind getting a place here instead of his current dump.

A few weeks after the copper wire incident, it had stayed pretty quiet in the area, Roger's heightened sense of security faded, and he went back to just being "normal" again.

As Roger made a sweep of the building, he approached the 4th floor and headed toward his favorite lookout spot. It was almost 6:00 a.m., and the world's light switch was starting to become less dim as the minutes rolled by. That's how Roger viewed it anyway. He imagined God built in a global light, the sun, and installed a dimmer that moved on its own. Right now, the dimmer was beginning to slide up. Although not very bright, the visibility was starting to improve.

Across the street from Roger, moving away from the water, was a row of local businesses that you could just tell needed life support to stay open. Chains and bars were in the windows for security reasons, which only made the whole area very unattractive.

This particular shift though, something looked different. The first few hours of Roger's shift were quiet, but when he looked down to the street, he noticed a dark-colored van that Roger could have sworn was not there before. As he examined the road, he saw no other vehicles, and as he listened, he heard no noise. Thinking nothing more of it, he stepped away from the hole in the wall where a window would soon be and continued on his route through the building.

As Roger got around the corner, he heard a scream. Not able to make out what was being yelled, he hurried back to an open apartment with again, a hole for the window, and looked down. The back doors of the van were now open, and a young woman was kicking and trying to scream as two older-looking men desperately wanted to shove her in the back of the van.

She did her best to fight, but she was bound and could only kick and try and scream when her mouth wasn't covered by a hand of one of the men. She was wearing a red dress, and from the looks of it, had been out that night doing who knows what.

Roger, acting on instinct, yelled down at the men.

"Hey! You! Let her go!" Without waiting to hear or see anything more, he raced down each set of stairs, hurdled over piles of wood and wires, until he reached the southern entrance. Busting out of doors, he went to heroically save the young woman, but he was too late. The van had already fled, and there was no sign of the young woman.

In a panic, he grabbed his phone and dialed 911 to report what he had just witnessed. Roger's heart was beating out of his chest, his adrenaline was pumping, and he was in his element. This was his chance! This was it! This was his way in...his conscious smacked him in the back of the head and reminded him that a young woman was just abducted, but he pushed that aside...this was now his destiny, and he would stop at nothing to solve it.

Part 2
Dealing with Reality

The rest of Roger's morning was spent giving police as much detail as he could and also showing off, just a little, in front of the construction crew and, of course, the owner.

By the time his shift was over, the adrenaline had just worn off, as there was no one else to tell the story to. Roger's replacement arrived, punctual as usual and in time for Roger to head home.

During his drive, which was much longer than on his way in, and also during his shower and feasting time (that's what he called it), Roger replayed the event over and over in his head. There had to be something, a small detail, he was missing. There was something off about that van, and also, where did that girl come from? Why was she dressed like that? It reminded him of a dress that Lisa loved to wear when they went on select dates.

And then it hit him. It hit him so hard he slammed his legs against his kitchen table as he leaped from his chair in shock and disbelief.

Immediately grabbing his cell phone from the kitchen countertop, Roger dialed Lisa. "Come on...pick up already." Voicemail.

"Lisa, if you get this, please call me back immediately, please, I mean it!" Roger re-dialed a few more times to only get the same voicemail in his ear. "Hi, this is Lisa. Sorry I missed you, but it's because I'm single and ready to mingle...'kay bye!"

Roger detested the voicemail, but there wasn't anything he could do about that. What he could now do though, was begin to freak out. There was no actual proof it was her, and yes, she rarely took his calls, but a text back was never out of the question, and Roger's phone was not buzzing.

He has been given a card of a detective that handled these types of cases, the missing person files. He looked in his wallet for where he stashed it and made the next call to him.

"Detective Burns? Yes, hi, it's Roger from earlier this morning. Look, I know this might sound crazy, but I think the young woman that was grabbed was actually my ex!" Roger waited...

"Yes, of course, I'm serious. Why would I make that up?" The look on Roger's face now one of anger and disgust.

"Well, if you're not gonna go look for her, I will!" Silence.

Roger slammed his phone down. Not bothering with the rest of his plate of food, he went for his jacket and shoes, and got ready to head out. Next stop, Lisa's place.

Part 3
Clues, Clues, and Antonio

By the time Roger reached Lisa's apartment, he was feeding all kinds of emotions, and he didn't know which one would pop the cork first. He parked, jumped out, and ran up the flight of stairs on the outside of the building to her floor.

Lisa lived in a multi-unit apartment building that housed many apartments over a long stretch. Stairs on the outside of each end gave access to the long string of seven units, totaling fourteen with the bottom apartments added in.

Reaching Lisa's door, he pounded on it. "Lisa!" No answer. More pounding ensued. "Lisa, are you in there?!"

Just as he gave up hope, the door opened, the security chain stopping it from fully exposing the insides to Roger, and it wasn't Lisa standing there.

A tired looking, shirtless, tattooed punk who looked like he was in a deep sleep answered instead.

"Who the hell are you, and how do you know Lisa?" Before he allowed Roger to answer, he unchained the door to open it wider to reveal his full body, and his demeanor changed from tired to pissed in two-seconds flat. "And what do you want with her, forget your wallet did ya?"

While trying to answer all those questions at once, Roger also took an eyeball of what was happening in the apartment. The door made immediate entry to the living room. Within Rogers' view, he could see an older brown couch and a glass-topped coffee table sitting in front. On top of the table was a pistol, with the clip sitting out, bullets facing Roger and a small scale with some white powder in a baggy sitting next to it.

In a moment of fluster, Roger tried to pretend he didn't see the table and overly compensated by attempting to act casual.

"Hey, man—how's it going? My wallet, no? I was just wondering where she was...we were, uh, we were supposed to meet up for dinner tonight."

The mysterious man at the door crossed his arms and acted coy. "Really? Is that so? Well, I don't know where Lisa is right now..." He pulled a face trying to get a name...

"Oh, Roger. It's Roger. And you are...?"

"Oh, I'm Antonio. Lisa and I live together, and she never mentioned a Roger before. So I'm going to suggest that you run along and go have some dinner by yourself, Roger."

Saying this, he pulled out his knife and started twirling it around in a non-threatening way, but just enough to help Roger get the point.

Taking the hint, and removing his body that was leaning against the wall, Roger said nothing and turned and walked away. Antonio, being the observant man he was, stepped one foot out the door and watched him leave. Once Roger was out of sight, he put the knife back, and replaced it with his cell phone.

"Hey. It's me. We have a problem. The ex is looking for her, no one saw you, right?" A few moments later... "Yeah, well I'm sure he suspects something. He saw my powder on the table. I was just getting the next batch ready for tonight."

A few more words were passed through from the other end, and then he hung up just in time to see Roger drive away. Now Antonio knew what car he was driving as well as also knowing he was looking for someone who wasn't going to be found.

PART 4
TAKING ACTION

"Burns, is that you?"

"What do you want, Rogers? I have actual work to do today."

"Look, Burns. I just went over to Lisa's place..."

"The girlfriend? Sorry, ex-girlfriend?"

Not enjoying his tone, he replied, "Yes, my ex, her name is Lisa. Look, something fishy is going on over there."

"Please do tell, I'm all ears, Roger."

"Look. This other guy answered, and inside the apartment there was a gun and drugs and a scale sitting on the coffee table. Plus, he pulled out a knife on me while I talked to him. His name is Antonio."

"Did you get the last name there with that, genius?"

"Yeah, I asked him to spell it for me while I wrote it...No I didn't ask for his last name, don't be an ass, Burns."

"Okay, so he had a gun, could be legal, and something that resembled what you thought were drugs. What do you want me to do, raid the apartment because Roger said so?"

The detective was irate and rude to Rogers which only made Roger fierier than usual.

"Look, detective," he said with a very sarcastic tone. "Lisa is missing, it looked like her when I saw the abduction, and this Antonio guy is suddenly in the picture with weapons and drugs. And you're telling me it's not connected?"

"Look, maybe it is, maybe it isn't. I tell you what Rogers, I'm gonna do you a solid." His tone softened. "I know you've had it rough. I know you applied to be a cop and you barely missed the cut for the academy. So I'm gonna help you out, okay?"

"I'm listening." Roger was also now calmer. "And it's just Roger by the way...not Rogers."

"Okay, yeah, sorry. Look, Roger, I am going to send a car to sit on Lisa's apartment for the rest of tonight and tomorrow to see if something shows up. If you're lucky, she was just out with her head in the clouds, and she's fine—minus the poor choice in men. If not, then we will look into it more. But you have to promise me that you stay away from her apartment!"

"Yes, yes, good, I can do that. Just promise me you will call if you see Lisa, please!"

"Uh-huh, sure thing." And then the phone went silent.

Roger wasn't sure what to do next. Going home was going to be useless, even if he was drained. He would typically have tried to sleep a few hours by now, but it was pushing 5:30 p.m., and he hadn't even touched a pillow.

Deciding that going home wasn't an option, he instead went back to his workplace. Only when he arrived, he parked down the street a half block from the building he watched, keeping an eye on the same spot where Lisa was taken. There was no doubt in his mind it was her being shoved into that van, he just didn't know why. Antonio was the connection, but he couldn't go back to the apartment, so he just waited— hoping for a clue.

The street Roger was parked on was barely used considering there was nothing industrial about the place anymore. Storefronts that sat on the street Roger was parked on were no longer in business, and only one bar was open on the weekends in this neighborhood, and it wasn't exactly the kind of bar you just decided to go try on a limb either.

Hours had passed. Roger had fallen asleep, arms at his sides and his mouth open. What woke him was the loud claps of thunder overhead. Startled, he took in his surroundings, trying to figure out why he was asleep in his car. Lightning lit up the now very dark sky, and then he saw it. The only place that was open on the weekend—"River Front Bar."

It was pouring cats and dogs, and even though Roger wasn't exactly dressed for a night out, that didn't stop him from getting out and running across the street and around the corner to where the bar stood proudly. Or as proud as it could for its shady reputation.

Roger heard rumors and stories from some of the construction workers about what went on inside of there on the weekends. It wasn't a place a regular guy wanted to mess with. Going up the two concrete steps, Roger pushed open the wet, wooden door and stepped into the dry, but loud bar.

While Roger was taking in his surroundings, his cellphone began to ring. Roger wouldn't answer though because he managed to leave it in his car, and of course, the only person calling him at this point was none other than Detective Burns. A voicemail and text arrived soon after, both sitting untouched for the time being.

Inside the bar, Roger had made his way to the bartender and asked for a beer, at least to fit in. When the bartender came back, Roger leaned in above the noise to ask a question.

"Hey, have you seen a gorgeous blonde in here recently? Probably wearing an amazing red dress...like, way too fancy for this place? No offense..."

"Come to think of it, yeah I did see her the other night. She comes in a lot actually. What's her name?"

"Lisa. Her name's Lisa."

"Oh, Lisa? Why didn't you say so? Yeah, she helps out a lot with our 'regulars,' but she hasn't been in and I've given her shifts over to Stacy."

Pointing to the far left, and back of the bar, there was an apparent bouncer blocking an entryway to who knows what. Roger, being the brilliant guy he was, went over.

"No one gets in here unless you're paying."

"Oh, yeah, of course, I'm paying," Roger said, a little confused. He reached for his wallet.

"Tonight, it's a Benjamin to get in."

"A hundred bucks?" said an alarmed Roger.

"If you don't like it...leave, or I'll help you leave."

"No, no I want in." Roger pulled the last of his cash from his wallet and handed it to the big man at the door.

"Have a good time." He smirked as he stepped aside.

Upon squeezing past the bouncer, Roger was met with dark walls and a style of music. The air smelled cleaner compared to the actual bar crowd, and the narrow hallway turned a few different ways until he reached a new opening. This time there was no money hustler waiting, but instead, the doorway was lined with red, shiny beads as though to form a curtain.

Poking his hands and head through, Roger stepped in and found an exotic-looking woman staring back at him from a stripper pole.

"Stacy?"

"That's right, baby. You've come to the right place...why don't you have a seat and let me take really good care of you."

Playing along, Roger sat down on the overstuffed couch while Stacy began dancing around the pole. She was dressed in nothing that needed explaining as it left zero to the imagination for Roger.

Trying to focus on why he was there, Roger spoke up in conversation.

"I thought Lisa was working tonight?"

Spinning around again to face Roger, Stacy kept her routine going but at least engaged with him. "She normally would be, but she's been 'retired.'"

"What do you mean, retired?"

"All I know, baby, is that she asked the wrong questions to the wrong people, and now she's gone."

While Stacy and Roger were getting to know each other over an awkward conversation, in the central bar area, Antonio was present and in control.

The bartender filled Antonio in on what was going on with Roger and his current whereabouts. Antonio decided it was time to give Roger a retirement party too.

"Have Danny bring the van around. It's time Roger went to see Lisa."

Part 5
Good Cop, Dead Guy

Burns put a cell trace out on Roger's phone to figure out where he was. Sure enough, to his worst nightmare, he knew he was close to the bar which only meant more bad things to come.

He tried calling Roger again. "Roger, get out now. That Antonio guy is bad news, he's gang connected and one of the bad ones...call me right now."

He knew there was no use, and time was running short. Leaving Burns with no choice, he put on full lights and sirens and sped to the bar in the riverfront district where he knew, or at least hoped, Roger still was.

It didn't take long to find his car parked there, but Roger was nowhere to be found.

Meanwhile, Roger had been showed the polished end of a handgun, the same one he saw on the coffee table and was hurried out the back of the club and into a dark van.

"So this is what you did with Lisa. Shoved in here and then killed her?"

Antonio didn't respond with words, only a sly smile which just made Roger more afraid of what might be next. The doors slammed, and Roger was held at gunpoint while Danny drove the van. The van went right past the detective, and when Burns saw the plates, he called in for immediate backup and tailed the van.

The van followed a path along the river that would eventually lead to another set of docks, also neglected over the years. Roger was forced out and was pushed toward the edge of the dock.

The smell was irreplaceable. Rotten wood and trash mixed together filled his nose and intruded his headspace. But the real danger was not the toxic water, but more so the .44 caliber bullet waiting for him in Antonio's gun.

"Look, before you shoot me and dump me in this nasty ass water, at least give a dying man one last question."

"And what might that be?" Antonio asked as he wafted the gun around.

"Why. Why'd you kill Lisa, she didn't deserve to die, so why'd you do it?"

"I guess that is the only question that counts, right? And you might as well know since you will soon be joining her.

Lisa left you and found herself alone in my bar. So after a few free drinks, I introduced her to a way of making enormous amounts of cash. She accepted, but then she tried to steal from me. That night that you yelled for me to stop...she was coming to you for help, did you know that? She ran...but we caught her before she could get to you. I don't know, I guess she thought you could protect her..."

Antonio's cruel story made him laugh, which also made him off guard.

While all the bantering had been going on, Roger had seen Detective Burns approaching, with his own pistol drawn and ready. The question of why, he figured would be too good to pass up, and during that time, Burns had managed to sneak up and get close enough to Antonio without being noticed.

"Well, Antonio, I guess you shouldn't kill me after all that."

"Oh?" Antonio was laughing more. "And why is that?"

"Because you assumed I was alone..."

Antonio turned around, his gun still pointing out, and then four shots rang out, each one feeling louder than the shot before it. Antonio dropped to the ground, and Danny got on his knees with his hands behind his head.

"Boy, am I glad to see you!"

"You're lucky you're alive, Roger. But I am also lucky that you didn't give up. We haven't found Lisa yet, but it's only a matter of time."

Roger began to walk away, his car being many blocks from their current location.

"Roger..." Burns said with a smile. "Take that exam again...you might surprise yourself."

Roger smiled slightly, and gave a little head nod before continuing on his way back to his car.

About six months later, Roger came back to the bar that almost got him killed and again, sat and ordered a drink. "Stacy working tonight?"

"Yes, she is...I believe, if I am correct, you already know the price."

"Oh, I sure do..."

"Everyone, freeze! You are under arrest for prostitution and money laundering!"

Roger pulled out his badge from behind his shirt, and a swarm of cops in full tactical gear swarmed the bar, including the back room. Sure enough, Stacy was there, scared out of her mind, sobbing.

Roger took over for the officer and instead of cuffing her, he escorted her outside and told her that this was for Lisa.

"I couldn't save Lisa that night. But I can save you now."

Stacy sobbed, stretched out her arms, and hugged Roger tightly. She kissed him and then turned and ran away from her nightmare.

Roger felt pretty good about what just happened, and as he looked upon this unprecedented night sky, he could have sworn he saw a start wink at him as if it were Lisa looking down and approving what he just did.

That bar never saw another open night and the new construction was almost ready to open. He grabbed a tenant application and walked away, happy, content, and a cop after all.

The End.

Pete "Funny Bone" Wells

Part 1
Crossing Paths: The Beginning

Like any good story, there is a beginning, a middle, and an end. And, with any story worth telling, there is a twist of fate. This particular twist, however, is not mine. In fact, I am not even the main character in this story; I am merely the storyteller.

The person I will tell you about is that of someone who has many tales to tell. But why should he be the one to tell them? Does a prince open his door, or does someone open the door for him? Does the president drive, or does he have a limo driver? If a story is that great—the storyteller is anyone and everyone willing to speak.

And I guess that is where I came in. You see, it wasn't that long ago that I met the man we now know as "Funny Bone." But before he was nicknamed "Funny Bone," he was called by any common name...Pete. Pete Wells, to be exact.

Pete and I grew up in a little town in Iowa. Most people don't even know where Iowa is, and if they do, they first think it's Ohio. This particular detail isn't that important, but it did make me laugh on occasion when trying to explain to people where we were from. But what does make this significant, is a simple fact that it doesn't matter where you live, or grew up, or even end up...the world isn't big enough to hide from fate.

Pete and I were strangers on a path of great opposites. Nevertheless, fate brought us together and looking back now, some many years later, I still don't know, or understand, how this happened—but I am very glad it did.

My name is Jordan. I only say that so that you are not confused as I tell this tale. I would hate to have you think I was someone else entirely.

Pete was a typical kid growing up. He had parents, family, he went to school...he even had a job working at the local grocery store as a bag boy and sometimes working the register. He was by all means normal. Run of the mill, you could say.

I, on the other hand, am a few years older, with already being out of college, I worked at a bank in the same town. Every so often, I would see Pete come into the bank to deposit his checks and withdraw money. He was smarter than the average kid too. I could usually con customers into opening up new credit cards, but Pete knew better than to get involved.

And this is how things went on for a little while. It wasn't until financial trouble hit me, that I decided to make a life altering decision. I decided I should join the USAF, the United States Air Force. After meeting with a recruiter, and taking the ASVAB test, which helped determine I was at least smart enough to get in, I signed on the bottom line to enlist.

I did promise this story wasn't about me, so let me bring you up to speed on Pete. He enjoyed his role at the grocery store, but for some reason couldn't help think that he should do more with his life. One could argue that he still had a ton of life left to live. He hadn't even started college officially. That was supposed to happen in the fall. I say supposed to, because as you may have guessed by now—that didn't happen.

I can't say his parents were thrilled about the idea, but they didn't stop him from pursuing a new direction, which is of course, how our paths crossed. He also joined the USAF.

If Pete had been older, I guarantee he could have gone straight in as an officer. But, not having the degree needed, he enlisted just like me. He passed his ASVAB with high scores and could be almost anything he wanted in the

Air Force, but no matter what, he was going to basic training, just like me down in San Antonio, Texas.

This is where our story really begins. And let me just say...being called "Funny Bone," came at quite the price for him, me, and the rest of our street flight.

Part 2
Keep Texas Flat: The Middle

I have to say that Basic Training turned out to be no joke. At least, to the other fifty-seven trainees it was no joke, but to Pete, everything turned out to be an opportunity for a good laugh. The only problem was, that laugh came at the expense of everyone else.

Take for example one "funny" day where some of the trainees had screwed up, including Pete, and made everyone suffer for it. We had been in the dining hall and this trainee, Evans I think was his name, he managed to drop his food tray all over the floor. Perfect. It was lunch time, we had already done a lot of running that morning, and this little incident wouldn't make our day any better.

So, of course, our instructor, Sgt. Winters was all too happy to make us suffer for it. But what made it worse, was Pete didn't see that Evans dropped his tray in time, and walked right through it and falling over. And because one other trainee was there and did nothing to help, well all three were in trouble now.

If dropping the tray wasn't funny enough (at least when I think back now), what Pete said shortly after just blows me away even to this day. Our instructor made everyone get up from their seats and stop eating and told us that familiar line of, "We better help keep Texas flat! Start pushing!" and blew his whistle.

Right on cue, without missing a beat, here comes Pete with a stupid comment that just makes me smile every time I reflect on that day. He goes, "Sir, Trainee Wells reports as ordered. Sir, shouldn't we be pushing outside if we're gonna make sure Texas stays flat?" I'm quite sure my heart stopped working for a few seconds when I heard him say it. Our instructor was pissed, to say the least. And outside we went. That afternoon was miserable...and Pete was now known as "Funny Bones" and was called that every day since by Sgt. Winters.

But that was Pete. I still, to this day, don't know how he managed to graduate training and move on, but he did. We both did. This is part of the story, for me though, where I have to change gears. Pete and I went off to different tech schools for our training. Pete became a pilot, and I was a load master for the C-17 planes.

I had been working my way to a load master and had finally achieved that goal when not six months later I hear a familiar voice in my headset. As you probably guessed, it was none other than our funny man, Pete Wells. Pete had decided that he wanted to fly the big dog and ended up piloting the C-17 that I was working on. Of course, these birds don't just get one pilot, so he did have his own crew of people to work with, but as the load master for this plane, I was in constant communication with those pilots.

I remember one morning, I think it was about 05:00, and we were about to leave for a drop in

Afghanistan. They needed supplies, and this mission was going to be a long one. I am going over the load calculating weights etc. when out from the cockpit comes this smug guy with a cheesy grin on his face. Captain Wells. He approached me and said, "If we don't get this bird in the air soon, we're gonna end up sinking Texas instead of keeping it flat...okay?"

All I could do was chuckle and tell him, "Yes, sir." He smiled. And then just walked back. Sadly though, that was one of the last times I really smiled like that, as I don't recall too many more jokes coming out of Pete's mouth once we were up in the air.

Radio chatter was minimal. I never did get the chance to ask him what was bothering him that day. Maybe he knew how it was going to end...perhaps in some small way, he had seen the future and somehow had expected what was coming. I suppose it doesn't make any difference now though. It's just me, telling you a story of this funny guy.

Even the best of comedians have to stop telling jokes eventually...

Part 3
Broken Wings: The End

As I stand here and tell you this story, I cannot help but be emotional. At the same time, I hear the voice of our Instructor, Sgt. Winters, as he would always tell us to keep our emotions hidden, and to continuously hold ourselves firm. For some reason, of all the things our Instructor said, that one stood out the most.

I suppose in a way it made things easier. Notably easier when the shots rang out, and the bullets flew. As for the "where," I still to this day am not allowed to say, but I can for sure say who. Pete and I were on the ground. I was getting gear unloaded from our plane, and the new base that was being built from the ground up in a hostile environment came under attack.

There was one high ground point that was just close enough to our new base that would be a point we needed to control as soon as possible. I don't know if the intel we received was bad, or if we just got unlucky that day, but taking that vantage point was never going to happen—at least not with the forces we had available when the attack happened.

An overwhelming spray of AK-47 fire and the occasional RPG came hurling down on top of us. The cover was minimal and taking the upper hand seemed impossible. Even though I was with the plane at the time, I did what I could by firing back, but with an exposed rear entrance I was out in the open essentially. I took a bullet to the leg, which dropped me instantly.

Pete, the funny guy that he was, yelled at me, "What the hell are you doing laying down? This ain't the beach in Mexico!"

Even though I was hurting, the adrenaline and the sound of the "Funny Man" certainly helped block that immediate shock.

Pete grabbed me. He exposed himself and shouldered his weapon so that he could help me. I'll never forget what happened next...

As we moved away from the plane over to where the suitable cover was available, we heard on a radio call for fighter jets to swoop in and light the hill top up on a bombing run. It wasn't more than six minutes before a couple of C-10s roared in and lit that place up like the 4th of July.

Those six minutes felt like a long time though. I stayed hunkered down as best as I could. I never wanted to admit it, but I closed my eyes and just prayed I would survive this ordeal. Pete never left my side.

It wasn't until I heard the C-10 planes rush in that I knew I would be okay. As soon as they passed, the shooting stopped. The threat had been eliminated...it was all over.

We lost five guys in that fight. It didn't last more than one hour in total...but one of those five is the reason we are gathered here today. Pete never left my side because he was severely injured, and ended up bleeding out. I won't say more, as this is not the place.

It turns out that Pete hadn't just saved me. You see, I thought he never left my side, as I just said...but in fact, that wasn't Pete next to me at all. That was Levinsky. He had also been shot, he was hurt for sure, but he was still alive. And then next to Levinsky was Whitts. Pete Wells had saved three of us in that time.

Once I realized Pete wasn't next to me, I crawled out from my covered position...looked across the flat, dirt ridden ground and saw Pete laying there. At first, I thought he was just laying down to catch his breath. I yelled out to him. He didn't respond. I yelled again, louder—nothing.

The third time, it was as if the sound was stuck in my mouth. In my head, I was screaming for him, but nothing came out. If you saw me at that moment, I probably just looked cold and broken.

Pete was a funny guy, for sure. Because of him I can stand here today and look down upon my family. And Pete, he can look down on all of us from Heaven.

To Pete... May your wings never be broken. We salute you...

The End.

Waking Forest

It was once foretold,
that a treasure of gold
was sitting inside a hill.

Whomever so brave
should take it away,
wouldn't live to see the next day.

Introduction

Today

Welcome! My name is Murphy. My friends call me Murph. I know why you're here. You want to know more about the mystery treasure inside the Hills of Fire. The truth is, I don't know all the answers to your questions, but I can at least tell you a story that I do know. But for that story, you must first understand how we came to live here.

Isn't it a beautiful summer day? Only a few white clouds sail the skies, leaving behind no trace of their existence. If you listen closely, you can hear the luscious, green grass whisper as the warm air dances through the blades.

The trees, while holding tightly to their leaves, sway, and the sound of children running around and hiding amongst them always fills your ears. It is, in fact, a perfect summer day.

Not far from the grassy field is a forest. But this is no ordinary forest. This is our home, Waking Forest. Although it is true that I, along with the others, once lived in a prospering village. We were happy people with much to share and give...at least until someone went exploring. That was a day that no one here will ever forget.

Of course, no one can tell the tale of what happened quite like Marcus, because after all, it was he that ventured into the Hills. But he never did say how he survived; he would only tell us of his journey home. And that is where our story begins. The tale of Marcus coming home.

Part 1
The Hills of Fire

Six Months Ago

"Marcus, I hope your sword is as still sharp. You did say no one has made it out of here alive before." Marcus simply stared forward as he faced danger head-on.

With him, was a slender man who was no stranger to the evils of these lands. Anton was his name. Excellent with a bow, and with the ladies, due to his charming personality and chiseled looks. He killed the dragon that dwelled in the Eastern Mountain and helped the Oakenshires defeat the trolls. And now, he faced an unknown foe—but scared he was not.

Marcus, however, was quite afraid. He knew the rumors as they were always told to the children growing up, warning them of imminent doom if they ever decided to venture to the Hills of Fire. Marcus grew into a fine man and was a blacksmith by trade. He worked hard and took pride in his work, but it was never enough.

While staring at the Hills of Fire, Marcus relived a memory of home, the village tavern where he sat with friends.

Music played, and beer was passed around. Villagers laughing and smiling everywhere, except for Marcus. Marcus was sitting on a long, wooden bench in the corner so that he could see out. The bench was firm and hard on his overworked body, but the ale was smooth and refreshing. As he took another drink from his cup, he was joined by some locals.

"Marcus! Good to see you, chum! How the heck are you?" Marcus received a firm smack on the shoulder. The man now sitting to his front was Jacob, the grain farmer. Also, a very hard working man, with a family to feed and lots of animals to tend to. Without skipping a beat, Michael showed up and plopped himself right next to Marcus on the bench.

"Hey, fellas! Quite the row in here, isn't it!" Michael was the local baker, but he also traveled to nearby villages to sell his bread. He was a very profitable man, and oddly, didn't drink—but he would always be in the tavern.

Marcus sipped his drink and acknowledged the two men in front of him. "I'm glad you're both here. I was going to come and find you tomorrow, but I need to speak with you now, if you don't mind."

The loud tavern muffled his words a little, but Michael and Jacob had no problem hearing him. They could see the seriousness in his face. So Marcus, having their attention, leaned in and the other two followed.

"I need to borrow one of your carts, Michael, and two of your bulls, Jacob."

A confused Jacob piped up. "What for, Marcus, are you selling your work now too, like Michael?"

Jacob gestured toward Michael when he said this, and Michael was eager for more understanding.

"No. I'm not selling anything. I..." Marcus quickly looked around to make sure no one was dropping in on their conversation. "I'm going on a trip, and I need them to make the journey. It's too far for me to walk."

Michael now took his chance to ask, "Where are you going, Marcus? Why all the secrecy?"

Marcus paused, took a large drink of his ale, and then just let it out. "I'm going to the Hills of Fire." He whispered this as low as he could without having to repeat himself.

Jacob smacked his leg on the table as he about jumped up from his seat. "You're going to the Hills of Fire!?" he said with a little too loud of a voice. Marcus immediately grabbed his arm and pulled him back down.

"Do you want everyone to hear this!? Yes, that's where I'm going. I know it's basically forbidden and I wouldn't normally do it, but I need to go. I can't explain it, I just need to go. Can I rely on you? I leave first thing tomorrow."

Michael looked at Jacob. Silence spoke volumes, but finally, Michael answered. "Yes, Marcus. You can count on us."

Marcus remembered that moment like it happened yesterday, but it had been months since that conversation happened. And now, with his trusted friend, he was ready to face evil.

Part 2
A Time to Reflect

As the two brave, or foolish, men faced the hill, the sun was setting in the distance. The name "Hills of Fire" was an understatement; it was more like a mountain.

The jagged edges and steep slopes, with the top of the mountain seemingly out of view, combined with the ever-growing darkness made Marcus feel uneasy about this decision. But he had come this far. Turning back now would be a waste, and he couldn't quit.

The two of them decided to rest for the night. They gathered wood and started a fire. The animals were released from their ropes and tied up to a tree where they could rest. There wasn't much banter between the men, but that's probably because they were both thinking about what tomorrow might bring.

Marcus, after a long silence, finally spoke. "Carson...do you think we will make it out alive?"

Carson was stoking the fire to keep it going a little while longer. The mountain may have blocked the wind, but it was still colder than they would have preferred.

"Sure, why wouldn't we? We have no idea what to expect in there—there could be nothing," Carson said with a confident look about him.

Marcus put down his flask and leaned toward Carson. "What do you mean, nothing? No one else has ever come out of there alive. People have gone, but no one comes home. What is to say that our fate is any different from theirs?!"

With his confidence now subdued, Carson could only nod in agreement, but he did offer up one piece of hope. "At least there are two of us..."

"You're right. I'll let you go in first, and if I see what kills you, I will run back and tell everyone!" Marcus said, laughing. Carson joined in. The mood may have lightened at the moment, but the truth would eventually stare them down.

"At least we've made it this far. You were pretty handy with your blade on our journey here, Marcus. Those bandits were very eager to take our livestock and all our goods."

"Thanks." Marcus smiled a little and looked into the fire. As he gazed upon the dancing flames, he thought back to that day.

***

4-Months Ago

"Carson look out! Bandits!"

An arrow flew beside the head of Carson and slammed into a nearby tree. From the bushes, three men came screaming out with swords raised high. Carson immediately jumped from the wagon and knocked down one of the bandits.

Marcus, being caught off guard and unprepared, didn't move and panicked instead. The other two bandits grabbed Marcus and threw him to the ground. One of them, jumping toward him with his sword ready to spear Marcus, landed in the wrong place. Marcus' sword had pointed straight up from the fall which ended up impaling the bandit.

Carson, who was finishing slaying the first bandit, turned to see Marcus pulling his sword out of the lifeless body. The third bandit, seeing he was outnumbered, dropped his sword and fled.

Carson and Marcus climbed back up on the wagon and collected themselves.

"Well done, Marcus. I had my doubts, but I can see you can handle yourself."

"Thanks, yeah it was, well, you know, he had it coming." Marcus knew he did nothing, and if it wasn't for the fall, he would have been the one laying on the ground in a pool of blood, not the bandit.

"You're just being modest. It's a good thing you found me, though. Who knows what else is out there."

"Marcus. Marcus? You with me?" Back to the present day, Carson had been talking to Marcus and was obviously not getting a response.

"Don't stare into the flames too long. You might get sucked in, friend!" Carson laughed.

"Yes, of course. Well, we should probably get some sleep. Tomorrow will be a long day no matter what happens. When we rise, we should let the animals go and make our way up the mountain. The entrance is supposed to be near the top...I think."

Both men grabbed their leather sacks and used them as pillows. With each as close to the fire as possible, it wasn't long before the warmth put them to sleep.

What they didn't know was that the fire had invited eyes from the mountain. They were no longer alone.

Part 3
The Inner Journey

The next morning came quickly. With the fire gone with nothing but charred and broken logs to greet them, they rose to their feet, stiff and soar. Realizing their flasks were empty, Carson offered to go fill them at the nearest stream.

"If I don't come back in ten minutes, the Fairies got me first!" Carson said, laughing as he was walking away. Marcus chuckled, but the danger was becoming very real. He looked up at the mountain with a blank stare. He knew they were on foot from now on, but danger felt closer than ever. A chill crawled down his spine.

"Agh! Marcus, help!"

Marcus ran toward the sound of Carson. Quick dashes between trees until the creek came into view.

"Carson! Where are you!?"

Just then, as Marcus darted into the stream, Carson began laughing from behind a bush.

"You should have seen your face! Oh my goodness, you looked horrified..." Carson kept laughing as he fully emerged from the bush.

"Hilarious, Carson." Marcus, climbing up the bank tried to dry himself off, but it was useless.

"Did you at least fill up the flasks?"

"Yeah, here!" Carson tossed the full and heavy flask to Marcus.

"Come on, let's get to our gear and start the journey upward!"

As the two men ventured back toward their camping spot, two more eyes followed them. A creature from the mountain who had seen them the night before was lurking behind trees.

This creature was most easily described as a dragon. However, to those who have seen and fought dragons, there certainly were significant differences. Dragons could fly, this creature instead could leap great distances due to its wings.

Dragons in these lands would breathe fire. This copy-cat, however, was just as deadly with its own breath. A yellow-ish fog would fill a small room in mere seconds, and anyone breathing it in would die a painful death soon after.

Its body was scaly on the back with fur on the front. The head looked like a typical dragon but its tail was smaller. And even though dragons were usually quite large, this look-a-like never grew more than the size of a man.

This creature was commonly known as the Poisoner, but to those who knew it well, its true name was "prodogan." The prodogon watched as the two men ventured on their way.

The mountain, as steep as it was, at least offered any daring climbers ridges as a makeshift staircase. With just their leather sacks and swords, they began the slow climb to the opening.

"How far up do you think it is, Marcus?" asked Carson as he labored his breath.

"I've only heard stories, but those stories say it's only halfway up the mountain. Once we find it, that's where my stories run out."

"How delightful," Carson said with much sarcasm.

It was the middle of the afternoon by the time they had reached the entrance. A grand display of power and also an overwhelming feeling of doubt and fear came from the appearance of the open entrance. The jagged rock and darkness made the roof of the entrance look like pointy teeth that were ready to consume whole anyone or anything that dared enter.

"Well, this is it," Marcus said as he drew his sword. "Are you ready?" He looked over at Carson.

Carson took off his bag and grabbed a torch from inside, lighting it. He held it up in front of them. "I am now, let's go find some gold!" Seemingly unfazed by the task ahead, he entered the mountain first.

As they stepped inside, the darkness surrounded them. It was quiet and gut-wrenching. Each step sounded like rocks smashing together, no matter how hard they tried to remain silent.

The path lead them downward with some portions being thin and others quite wide. Eventually, they came to a ledge that overlooked a huge open area. Looking up, they could see stairs on the other side that led to the very peak, and below, they saw nothing but black.

"Throw your torch down. Let's see how far it goes." The words of Marcus seemed hollow in this vast opening.

Carson took a step back and then tossed his torch as far as he could. It flew into the air and then dropped like a sack of potatoes until it hit bottom. What neither Carson or Marcus expected was that upon hitting bottom, the torch landed just close enough to a river of oil which soon ignited with a loud roar.

They followed the light as flames could be seen all around the bottom of the mountain. The flames danced upward and showed them both the path ahead of them that would allow them to get to the bottom. And eager they were because now, they could see their prize.

Marcus ran first, followed promptly by Carson. The mountain floor was full of gold from one side to another. Statues, coins, chests and more lined neatly with huge piles just there ready for the taking. It almost seemed too easy.

Both men began to fill their pockets with as much gold as they could carry. Marcus still had his leather bag on him which he quickly dumped out the contents and began to fill it with as much glorious gold as he could carry.

"We have to get back and tell the others!" Marcus said with sheer excitement.

"Yes, my village will be pleased too. There are no monsters here, it's just scary stories to keep us home. I wonder why they didn't want anyone to know about this place?"

Once they were done grabbing all they could, they began the slow climb back up so they could get out of the mountain. What they didn't realize was who was already there, or as they were about to find out, *what* was already there.

Just before they reached the landing where they originally started, a creature from above dropped and blocked their path. Both Marcus and Carson froze out of fear.

It was tall and horrifying. It wasn't but a few moments later when it was joined by a smaller creature, the prodogon. Carson, coming back to his senses, dropped everything he was holding and drew his sword. He took a step forward and lifted the sword above his head, ready to strike at the prodogon, when he was suddenly stopped.

"Stop!" rang out a bellowing, deep voice from the much larger creature.

"It speaks..." whispered Marcus in disbelief. Carson, completely mortified of this new discovery did stop, lowered his sword, and sheepishly stepped backward next to Marcus.

This talking creature lowered its head. It was attached to a long neck that looked smooth until you got up close. Its skin was actually lined with razor sharp looking teeth that could slice anything it brushed up against.

Its feet were large but with only, what you might call, toes with long claws. The legs were short, and they held up a mighty body with large wings that could easily span half the length of the mountain.

With its head lowered, the green eyes pierced the souls of Marcus and Carson. And then, it spoke again.

"This is my treasure...do you dare try to take it from me?!"

The two men said nothing.

Part 4
Meeting Fate

Meanwhile, back in the town where so many were hard at work, gossip was quickly spreading. So much so that the elderly mayor needed to make an announcement. He grabbed his tall hat and stood in the center on a small, wooden stool, next to the well.

"Hear me, hear me!" he yelled as best he could. The women and children came closer, and the merchants left their stands to see what the fuss was about.

"I know you've all heard the rumors of Marcus heading to the Hills of Fire. I am afraid to say it is true." Gasps and mumbling between the shocked onlookers grew.

"I have spoken to Jacob, who has been worried sick—and he himself heard it from Marcus directly. He did, in fact, travel to the Hills of Fire. Now listen, listen here." The crowd grew in number and in volume as some showed signs of fear and others more like excitement.

"We are not sending a search party." The crowd became deadly quiet. "No one who has ventured there has ever returned, why do you think Marcus, our blacksmith, would do the same? I shall be giving him one more week to re-appear. If he does not...his property will be forfeited and his belongings handed out. That is all—go about your business!"

The mayor stared down toward the crowd as they slowly faded away. They looked mostly disappointed, although there were a few that looked upon his store with greed-filled eyes.

Back at the mountain, however, Marcus and Carson were facing nothing they expected.

"Mr. Dragon, sir, we just wanted to see why no one ever came back that visited your mountain," Marcus said sheepishly.

"Is that so...then why were you lining your pockets with all my gold?" The creature got very close to Marcus as he inhaled. "I can smell your fear, human. But since I doubt you will live much longer, it won't hurt for me to tell you why no one ever escapes."

The prodogon slithered around to the back of the men as if they weren't scared enough.

"For a hundred years, I have protected this gold, and I have never let one single coin leave my side. I knew you were here before you even started your climb...I see everything."

The creature stretched its wings enough to create a large gust of wind that almost blew the men over. At the same time, it also uncovered something that caught the eye of Marcus. To his left, Marcus noticed a glowing blade sticking out of a pile of gold. The handle was large and strung with gold spirals, the blade itself was double-edged and appeared to shine gloriously.

This gave Marcus an idea...

"Oh, great creature, do you have a name?" Marcus slowly sidestepped toward the pile of gold. Keeping his feet and legs together, he blocked the view of the blade.

"Surely someone as powerful and mighty as you that takes care of all this gold must have a name that scares anyone who dares enter here."

Marcus had picked up some coins and dropped them one by one as he spoke. The creature, amused by this display, shot up into the air, flew over the top of Marcus, knocking him down in the process and landed on top of the tallest gold pile there was.

Using this to his advantage, Marcus quickly took out his blade and replaced it with the glowing sword. It was longer, heavier but so much more impressive. He wasn't sure what the connection was, but he knew it was important.

Carson watched closely and as soon as his eyes landed on the blade, he knew exactly what it was. A Dragon Killer. This was no ordinary blade, as its ability was to penetrate the skin of a dragon. An ordinary blade has no chance of doing this, so as soon as Carson caught on to the plan, he chimed in.

"Yes, do tell us, oh great creature, what do we call you?" Carson bowed a little to show some sign of respect.

"Humans...always so fascinating. Fair enough. My name is Ozark. And your time has come."

The progodon raised its wings in preparation to attack Carson, but Carson, being the hero he was, quickly swung his sword from his side and thrust it upward along the body of the prodogon. Turning back around, he found the cut he had made and thrust his sword directly into the heart of the beast.

The prodogon fell backward, spilling over gold coins and statues. Meanwhile, Marcus had run toward the other side of the mountain where he had first seen the stairs. Ozark, who became furious, let out a bellowing roar and flapped its enormous wings to chase after Marcus.

Carson was soon following the footsteps of Marcus, and they were both climbing up the stairs. Ozark was closing in and stretched its claws to grab them both. Marcus grabbed his sword and swung toward one of the claws. Hitting what felt like solid steel, it took a small chunk off the creature and injured him.

"No, that's impossible. A mere sword cannot penetra..." Ozark stopped. "Unless...you found the sword of Quintark!" He let out another loud roar. Only this time, a portion of the mountain roof shook and rumbled. Large chunks cracked and separated from the ceiling and they plummeted toward Ozark.

Seeing their chance, Marcus and Carson fled out of the mountain as fast as possible. Running down the mountain without care for themselves, it wasn't long before they made it to the bottom.

The sky was no longer blue and peaceful, in its place were dark clouds, and heavy rain began to fall.

"We have to get out of here!" Carson yelled through the sound of rain and now thunder. But before Marcus could agree, the side of the mountain was beginning to crack and crumble. Ozark was making his way out of the mountain. For the first time in one hundred years, he was going to leave his gold behind.

Even though the animals had been set free, they were not far away. They had been grazing and resting but were now seeking shelter of their own from the storm. Marcus and Carson ran toward them and mounted them like horses. With nothing to lose and everything to fight for, they kicked the animals, and off they went. They raced as far as they could away from the mountain and Ozark, who was now almost free.

What they didn't expect, however, was running into more bandits. Marcus made no mind of them as he knew a worse fate awaited them if they stayed. The bandits, instead of trying to stop them, froze in their tracks as they heard the roar of the Ozark dragon. They were frozen in place. The dragon did not take long to find them and he scorched them with one fiery blow.

The journey Marcus had taken to arrive at the Hills of Fire had taken months. One reason was that he didn't know the way. The other was, of course, bandits, but the biggest reason was his doubt. Marcus was always second-guessing his decision to even attempt such a daring journey. He made many stops and built too many fires to count.

At the end of it all, this journey wasn't really about the Hills of Fire, but more so about who Marcus was.

Being a blacksmith was one thing, but Marcus always knew there was something more out there for him. He just didn't know what it was.

Once the two men had made up enough safe distance, they rested under a bridge. They were dry there, and at the very least, out of sight. They both agreed that even though a fire was just what they needed, it would draw too much attention.

They spent the night there, each taking turns to watch guard while the other slept. The animals, of course, were all too happy to lay and sleep, but the two men found rest hard to come by.

"One more day's ride, and we will be back at my village, Carson. This is going to change everything. You'll see."

"I hope you're right, Marcus. Because if Ozark finds us...it's all over."

Part 5

Marcus The Brave

With the rains gone and the grass green, Marcus and Carson fled as if their lives depended on it. Once they reached the outer limits of the village, they came across Jacob in one of his many fields. While tending to some of his cattle, Jacob looked up and saw Marcus coming.

He ran to the edge and jumped over his rickety fence. "Marcus! Marcus!" He waved him down.

"I can't believe it. You're alive! Did you make it to the Hills of Fire?"

Marcus, out of breath, stepped down, and Carson joined him. "Yes..." he panted. "Yes, we made it. Jacob, this is Carson, my trusted ally." Carson extended a dirty hand.

"A pleasure. You must be Jacob," Marcus interrupted.

"Look, we can all sit around and get drinks and talk all we want, but we have bigger problems right now.

We need to get everyone out of here!"

Before Jacob could ask why, that all-too-familiar roar came from the distance. Jacob, on the other hand, was clueless as to what was going on.

"What was that? That didn't sound friendly..."

Marcus and Carson had already begun running toward the village. "That's because it's not, Jacob!" Marcus shouted as he ran. Jacob was no fool; he left his herd behind and ran the same way they were.

Reaching the town center, Marcus began yelling for everyone to drop what they were doing and leave. But no one was listening.

"You need to leave! Right now! Everyone get out!"

The mayor heard the ruckus and came out to deal with it. "Now look, Marcus, we're glad you're back, but rules are rules...your store and your belongings are going up for auction."

"You think I care about that right now? We all need to leave...now!"

"And why on earth would we do that, Marcus?"

Marcus turned and looked toward the sky, and then pointed. "That's why!"

A mighty roar bellowed from behind some trees, and within a second, Ozark could be seen as he scorched the earth with his fiery breath.

Everyone in the marketplace began to panic and run frantically, but Carson and Marcus stood their ground. With their swords now raised and ready to meet their fate, Ozark swooped down.

"How did he find us so quickly!?" Marcus muttered. "It's not like we have any of his..."

"Gold!" Carson shouted. "Check your pockets!"

Both Marcus and Carson filtered through their pockets and, sure enough, Marcus found two gold pieces still in his pocket.

Ozark was busy burning every building he could until his attention was caught.

Marcus flicked a piece of gold into the air, and Ozark went straight for it.

"How wise of you, human. Although I do believe you have one more that belongs to me. Should I take it from your charred corpse, or will you hand it over now?"

Marcus said nothing. Carson, who was now also panicking, looked at Marcus. But when he did, it was as if time were slowing to a halt right there. Marcus was not scared, panicked, or anything close to it. He was focused and fearless.

Marcus flicked the last remaining coin as high as he could into the air. With his sword in his hand, and with Ozark distracted, he leaped forward and plunged his sword into the dragon as deep as it would go.

Ozark let out a gut-wrenching screech as he fell back with the sword sticking out of him. Desperately trying to flap his wings, he got himself into the air.

"This won't be the last that you've heard of me..." And then he was gone.

**

Present Moment

"So there you have it," Murphy said as he grabbed his pipe to smoke. "That is how we ended up living here. Ozark The Dragon may return one day, but we will be ready. Thanks to Marcus and Carson who have had first-hand experience with the creature, we have set up some nice defenses—we'll be ready next time."

With those final words, Murphy stood up from his perch on a broken branch and headed back into the woods to join the others. Everyone in the area was busy going about their lives, cooking, sewing, hammering, and scraping.

This is after all why they call it...the Waking Forest!

THE END

About the Author

Jason Atkinson lives in the Midwest with his wife and son. This is Jason's second fiction book, and fifth book overall. Writing brings a lot of joy to Jason, but the bigger impact for him is when he gets feedback from his readers that they cannot wait to read more!

Made in the USA
Middletown, DE
09 December 2022

17727726R10106